ACCIDENTAL VEGAS BRIDE

ROSE MARIE MEUWISSEN

Print ISBN: 978-1-954030-02-2
Published in the United States of America
Nordic Publishing
Edited by Leanore Elliot
Cover Design by Rose Marie Meuwissen

nordic
PUBLISHING

❀ Created with Vellum

To my daughter, Tiffany, and all the time spent in Las Vegas watching her show and the beautiful water fountain display in front of the Bellagio hotel.

ACCIDENTAL VEGAS BRIDE

After six years of dating and no marriage proposal, Alli broke up with Sam. Getting out of town, on the weekend of Sam's thirtieth birthday, wasn't in her plans. Surprisingly, it sounded like the right choice since it allowed her to be as far away as possible from Sam and Minneapolis on that specific date.

Vegas would do nicely.

It wasn't that Sam didn't love Alli, because he did. But, starting a family was a big commitment that he didn't think he was ready to make, just yet. Six months later, neither had made *the call* and his birthday simply wouldn't be the same without her. When Sam's best friend suggested celebrating his birthday in Vegas, he agreed.

Maybe then he could stop thinking about Alli for a few days. Anything can happen in Vegas! Surely there was some truth to the saying—*What happens in Vegas, stays in Vegas.*

ACCIDENTAL VEGAS BRIDE

By

Rose Marie Meuwissen

CHAPTER 1

"This is going to be fun. Right?" Alli asked as she closed her suitcase.

"We *are* going to have the time of our lives," Susie answered, pulling her suitcase toward the door. "And don't forget, what happens in Vegas, stays in Vegas."

"Time of our lives? I could certainly use that but I will settle for fun," Alli stated. She lifted her suitcase off the bed and rolled it over to the door.

"We are going to have fun, you can count on it. Ready?" Susie asked and opened the door. They walked out to the garage and loaded the suitcases in the trunk.

"Are you sure we have everything?" Alli asked while she mentally tried to go over all the things she packed, in case she'd forgotten anything.

"Sure enough. If we forgot something, we can get it in Vegas."

They both got in the car. Susie backed the car out of the garage, drove down the street taking the entrance ramp onto the freeway.

"Right. Okay, fun it is!" Alli said.

"And don't forget, what happens in Vegas, stays in Vegas," Susie repeated.

"Of course, you know that isn't true."

"Well, if it isn't, it should be," Susie stated. "All kinds of crazy things go on in Vegas. People do things they would never even think of doing at home."

"I could never do something I wouldn't be able to talk about the next day."

"Promise me you will let your hair down a little and try to have some fun at least," Susie suggested.

"Heaven knows, I need to relax and have some fun. After I broke up with Sam, I completely lost my desire to date again. It's especially hard when you are still in love with the person you just broke up with. But it is over and I need to move on. I know I need to, but it's so hard." Alli looked out the window at the Mall of America as they drove by at sixty miles an hour. Thank heavens they had a ten o'clock morning flight and hadn't had to get up in the middle of the night simply to catch a flight.

"There will be lots of men in Vegas," Susie offered. "Men looking for a good time. And that is what you need. Someone who will make you laugh again."

"You think I should find some guy and do what with him? Spend the night with him?" Alli asked.

"You're not a virgin or anything like that, so why not?" Susie asked.

"Because it's wrong. It's not good for anyone. Especially me. Having sex with a strange man is not going to happen. Trust me, it won't."

"Okay, you do whatever makes you happy and I'll do the same." Susie parked the car in the long term parking area at the airport.

They walked into the airport with bags in tow and proceeded to the security area to get in line. Once through the screening process which always was a pain, food was next on their list. They stopped at the French Meadows Café, purchased salads for later on the plane to go along with chocolate croissants for breakfast and then made their way to Caribou Coffee to get some much needed caffeine.

"Some days, having this cup of mocha cappuccino makes the

whole day worth getting up for," Susie said sipping her multi flavored highly caffeinated beverage of choice for the morning.

"I will give you that one." Alli sipped her mint chocolate flavored cappuccino as they sat and waited at the gate for their flight.

"It's too bad Jennifer and Kally had to take a later flight," Susie stated.

"They will only be a few hours behind us. We'll meet them at the Monte Carlo Hotel. We can go ahead and check in, change into our swimsuits and head to the pool. I told them we would be there as soon as we checked into our room. You okay with that?"

"Don't you want to gamble first? Maybe win a jackpot or two before they get there," Susie asked.

"First of all, the odds of winning any money in Vegas are slim to none. I'm not giving them my money for nothing in return. Hell, I'd rather get something for my money. That's why I'll opt for shopping over gambling."

"You are no fun at all!"

"Really? You do the math, have you ever came out ahead with how much you spent, versus how much you won?" Alli asked.

"Probably not. But it always feels good when you win a large jackpot. Well, maybe not large to some people but $1,000 is large to me. I usually come out ahead but not by much. Last time it was only by $100. It is by far better than coming out behind."

"That's one way to look at it."

"Fine. We can go to the pool first," Susie said.

"Don't sound so disappointed. The casinos are open all night but the sun goes down early this time of year."

Finally, they were in line to board and followed the other passengers to their seats. As they walked down the narrow aisle between the seats on the airplane, they pulled their suitcases behind them with their large purses resting on one of their shoulders.

The line boarding the plane moved slowly, so Alli took the time to scan the plane to see if she thought there were any good looking men on the plane she might be interested in even chatting with in person.

Unfortunately, she didn't find a single one. She really hoped Vegas would offer a better, more interesting selection choice.

Once they were in the air, they ate their goodies from the French Meadow Café. Reading on planes was one of Alli's favorite things to do. Although, she was a bit old fashioned and brought her paperback romance novel along to read. Someone deserved the wedding and the happily ever after even though it wouldn't be her.

Las Vegas airport was crowded and Susie insisted on stopping at a group of slot machines that greeted them as soon as they walked off the plane.

Alli waited patiently while Susie dropped a quick $20 in one and came up empty handed. Why Susie never learned, Alli had no idea.

Alli found herself checking out the men for the first time in six months. It had been six months and she needed to do this. One guy caught her appraising him and smiled at her. She wasn't sure she could do this. She kept on walking and didn't look back at him. It wasn't surprising she found herself looking for someone who looked like Sam. She knew she couldn't replace him, what she needed was to look for someone who looked totally different so she wouldn't be reminded of Sam every time she looked at him. Sam was perfect for her in every way except for the minor little detail that he didn't want to get married yet, or have a family.

Time was running out for her and he unquestionably didn't understand how her biological clock was ticking away and she didn't have that much time left. She had just turned thirty before they broke up and she had tried to make him understand she simply couldn't wait any longer. All he said was that he was sorry but he wasn't ready to start a family. Now to top it all off, today was Sam's 30th birthday. She had planned to have a big birthday party for him, in fact she'd already began planning it, never thinking she wouldn't be there for it.

Which was why she had finally agreed to go on this Vegas trip. She didn't think she could stay in Minneapolis tonight, knowing it was his birthday today and someone had probably planned a big 30th birthday bash for him. And she was not invited. Had she really thought she would be invited, as the ex-girlfriend? No, of course not. But she had really wanted to be there. She really wanted to be with Sam, but he hadn't called her since their break up. He had broken off all contact with her and since he hadn't called her, she refused to call him, which led to a Mexican standoff. Neither one of them had made the call.

Susie signed the paperwork for their car rental and they took the elevator down to pick up the car. Alli hadn't been paying attention to how the conversation had gone between Susie and the car rental agent, so needless to say she was quite shocked to find out their rental was a Mustang convertible.

"Really? What were you thinking Susie? A convertible?" Alli asked staring at the car.

"I guess they were really wiped out of cars, so this is what they gave us. It's our lucky day. I think we need to go hit the slots," Susie said.

"Of course you do," Alli said as they loaded the suitcases in the trunk of the Mustang and got in the car. She was silent while they drove to the hotel.

"You okay?" Susie asked. "You are awfully quiet."

"It's Sam's 30th birthday today," Alli stated.

"I totally forgot. You never said anything. That's why you agreed to come to Vegas isn't it?"

"Yes. I was afraid I would call him or do something much worse like going over to his townhouse," Alli stated.

"No chance of that happening now. Promise me you won't call him this weekend."

"I promise. It's over. He obviously hasn't changed his mind since he never called me."

They parked and checked in the hotel. Alli couldn't believe her ears when she heard the clerk offer Susie a suite since it was the only room they had available with double beds due to a large convention being held at the hotel. She then heard the desk clerk say if they were looking for single men, the convention attendees were 95% men. What were the odds? Maybe she would meet someone really nice this weekend if their lucky streak held up.

An hour later, they were at the pool in their already pre-tanned bikini clad trim bodies, stretched out on the chaise lounges with a couple of frozen strawberry margaritas surrounded by chair after chair filled with hot men.

CHAPTER 2

"Hey, where are you guys?" Kally asked when Susie answered her call.

"Are you checked in?" Susie asked.

"Just got to our room."

"Put on your suits and come down to the pool. You've got to see this," Susie said.

"See what?" Kally asked.

"Just get down here as fast as you can and you'll see." Susie disconnected the call.

Alli couldn't believe all the men at the pool. Ten men had casually approached them already and they'd only been there a little over an hour. What do you say to strange men? They'd been asked to go dinner with a group of them and Susie had agreed.

"About time you got here," Susie said to Kally.

"Wow, this is unbelievable! It's all guys down here," Kally replied trying to take in the immensely beautiful sight of six-pack after six-pack.

"You're staring," Alli said.

Kally and Jennifer spread their towels on their chairs then sat down as they watched two very hot guys walking towards them, stop right in front of their chairs.

"Susie, you didn't mention you were meeting friends at the pool." He extended his hand to Kally. "Sebastian. Pleased to meet you."

Kally shook his hand and said, "Kally." Then looked towards Susie. "Sebastian is a friend of yours?"

Susie laughed. "We've only just met. Sebastian and his friends invited Alli and me to join them for dinner tonight at The Palms Hotel."

"That's why I came over here. I wanted extend the invitation to you and . . ." He extended his hand to Jennifer.

"Jennifer. We'd love to tag along," she said looking towards Susie.

"Well then, we'll see all of you at seven. I'm looking forward to dinner," he replied and walked off towards his friends seated at the bar.

"They are hot!" Jennifer exclaimed. "Alli, are you okay with going to dinner with these men?"

"It's Vegas and we came to have a good time. Right?" Alli asked.

"I for one can't wait!" Jennifer said.

A few hours later, they debated over what dresses to wear. The dinner restaurant in the Palms was considered to be a dressy one. They each brought a couple of fancy dresses along, and oddly enough, they all ended up wearing sexy little black dresses with black high heels.

Susie drove the convertible over to the Palms where she valet parked the car.

The Valet quietly stood watching as tan sexy legs slowly emerged from the open car doors.

Susie handed her car keys to him. He gave her a valet ticket, then she turned and walked over to where her friends were waiting.

The four sexy women walked through the casino doors. Every hot blooded man in the vicinity watched as these beautiful women entered. Little did the women know that one of the men standing in the lobby recognized them.

~

SAM FINISHED TAKING his shower in his Palms Hotel room and dressed for the upcoming night on the town with his friends to celebrate his 30th birthday. His phone rang, so he picked it up and saw his friend Dustin was calling.

"Sam, you will never believe who just walked into the casino lobby!" Dustin said.

"Who?" Sam asked.

"Alli," Dustin answered.

"Are you sure?"

"Hell, yes! Even has her friends with her, Kally, Susie, and Jennifer," Dustin stated.

"Keep an eye on where they go. I'll be right down," Sam said as he hung up the phone and walked out of his room to the elevators.

Why on earth would Alli be here? She had planned on throwing him a big birthday bash for his 30th birthday. Before they broke up, that was. So she wouldn't have had any idea he was in Vegas with his friends. That is unless someone told her. And that was highly unlikely. It had to be a coincidence. It totally had to be, there simply wasn't any other explanation.

The elevator stopped on the casino level and he got out. He stopped frozen in thought. What did he think he was doing? They were broke up. He certainly didn't need to go running after her. What would he even say? He started walking again, and saw Dustin waiting for him.

"Sorry man, didn't mean to ruin your night. After all, it is your birthday. You deserve to have a good time tonight," Dustin said.

"Where did they go?" Sam asked.

"What are you going to do? The guys will be here in a few minutes to meet us. Let's just go down to the strip and hit the casinos there."

"Where did they go?" Sam asked again.

9

"The guys said not to tell you."

Sam was getting impatient. "Where did they go?"

"Okay. They went in the Oasis Steak House. They met some guys there and walked in with them. She's probably with someone. Let's get out of here." Dustin watched as the guys, Tyler and Kevin, walked toward them.

"So what do you want to do?" Tyler asked.

"Let's have dinner at the Oasis Steak House and then we'll check out the nightclub," Sam said.

Dustin, Tyler and Kevin glanced at each other, shrugged and followed Sam into the Oasis Steak House. They were seated immediately.

Sam spotted Alli at a large table at the end of the room. There were four guys at her table. Unfortunately, it was hard to tell if she was with anyone in particular. A dark haired guy was seated next to Alli and was desperately trying to put the moves on her, but she wasn't responding. Good, he thought. Maybe she wasn't dating anyone, yet.

"Sam. You're staring and it's completely obvious," Kevin said.

"Does it look like she's with that guy?" Sam asked.

"Why do you care? You broke up with her. Remember?" Tyler asked.

"She broke up with me because I wouldn't marry her," Sam stated.

"Man, you still in love with her?" Kevin asked.

"I just wasn't ready to have a kid yet."

"And now?" Tyler asked.

"Maybe."

"I don't think maybe was the answer she was looking for," Kevin said.

"I definitely don't like watching that jack-ass come on to her," Sam said.

"Then let's go somewhere else. God knows there are thousands of restaurants in Vegas," Kevin suggested.

At that moment, Alli got up to go to the restroom and turned his way. Their eyes met. Sam hoped he still looked handsome to her as he couldn't stop himself from staring back at her. He wished she was sitting next him and running her fingers through his hair like she used to do. Man, how he craved her touch. She faltered for a moment then walked his way.

Sam got up and walked towards her. "What are you doing in Vegas?" Sam asked.

"What are you doing in Vegas?" Alli asked.

"I'm here with the guys for my birthday."

"I'm here with the girls since I didn't want to be in Minneapolis because it's your birthday today," Alli explained.

"What a coincidence," he said.

"I guess so." She shrugged.

Sam looked over at the guys watching him and Alli's friends watching her. He was at a loss as what to do. Alli looked so hot and he wanted nothing more than to take her up to his room and ravish her body. That would be a birthday present he would never forget. "Can I interest you in meeting me after dinner for a drink and to talk?"

"We are going to the Oasis Club for drinks and dancing after dinner," Alli said.

"Later then," Sam said and walked back to his table.

Alli walked back to her table.

"So?" Dustin asked.

"What? She's out here with her friends. It's merely a coincidence. Let's order some food," Sam said.

They ordered steaks and drinks. God only knew how bad he needed a drink right now. He couldn't take his eyes off Alli or the guy sitting next to her. He definitely hoped the guy next to her had enough sense to keep his hands to himself. He hadn't been so sure about this whole coming to Vegas plan but this evening was turning out to be quite promising. The food came and he watched Alli the whole time. All he kept thinking about was having Alli in his bed tonight and he was prepared to do whatever it took. He'd been crazy to let her walk away from him when he was crazy in love with her. He'd basically gotten scared. Hell, having a family was a lot of responsibility and it scared the hell out of him. But Alli didn't. He'd been too proud to call her after she'd walked out on him. Actually, he thought she would call him the next day and say she'd changed her mind, but now six months had gone by. The whole thing was stupid and he intended to change the status of their relationship just as soon as they finished dinner. He wanted her and he would have her. This was going to be the best birthday ever!

CHAPTER 3

"So what did he say?" Susie got up as Alli neared the table and leaned toward her to ask.

"He decided to come to Vegas for his birthday with the guys," Alli replied.

"Wow!" Susie exclaimed. "What are the odds we would run into them? Do you have any idea how many people are in Vegas, staying at the hotels? And there are a lot of hotels out here, too."

"It's fate." Alli couldn't think of any other explanation.

"Did he say anything else?" Susie pressed.

"He wants to meet me later for a drink," Alli said.

"And you told him what?" Susie asked. "No, I hope."

"I didn't really answer him, I basically told him we were going dancing at the Oasis Club after dinner," Alli explained.

"Alli. You can't let him get to you," Susie warned.

"My heart is racing. I'm still so attracted to him."

"Alli, you can't meet him." Susie shook her head. "He totally wants to have sex with you tonight. To celebrate his birthday and all."

"So. It's been six months without any sex. Sounds good to me." Alli shrugged.

"Oh, I'm sure it sounds great." Susie nodded. "And make up sex is always hot as hell. The problem is you're still in love with him. Tomorrow morning when he says, 'Thanks, I had a good time, but still not getting married,' then what?"

"I know, I thought about that. But—"

"But what? Maybe he'll have changed his mind and wants to get married and have kids now? The odds on that happening are slimmer than you winning a jackpot on the slots, which is probably about one in a million."

"I at least want a chance to talk to him anyway." Alli ended the conversation and took her seat at the table just as their dinner was being served.

Susie followed.

The guy, Dallas, sitting on the other side of Alli, struck up a conversation as if nothing out of the ordinary had just happened to her. He was definitely attractive and from his conversation, it seemed obvious he was well educated. He was a dentist but seemed to be well versed in any topic and it appeared he was interested in her. If Sam wouldn't have been seated at the table across the room, she may have very well been interested in him. But unfortunately for everyone concerned, she couldn't stop thinking about Sam and all the wonderful things he could do to her body. He could make her blood run hot, fill her body with passion and they could have wild un-abandoned sex. She felt the blood run to her cheeks as she thought about it. Poor Dallas probably thought he was turning her on.

Alli tried to focus on her steak dinner instead, a filet mignon and extremely tender. They would be doing more drinking than she was accustomed to, thus she ate so there would be some food in her stomach to absorb the alcohol.

The conversation strayed to all the sites and things to do in Vegas which were interesting since she hadn't been to Vegas for a while. She definitely wanted to see the Circe du Solei show at the Wynn. The acrobats in the show were said to be phenomenal.

The guys offered to take all four of the ladies to see it. Immediately, Susie agreed to go on behalf of all of them.

Before she knew it, they were leaving and walking over to the

Oasis Club. She looked over towards Sam's table and caught him watching her. He nodded but she had no idea what that meant. She hoped it meant he would see her over at the Oasis Club. She wasn't about to go running after him, so if he was interested, he needed to find her at the Oasis Club. And then, she would be all his for the night.

The Oasis Club emulated pure class with marble floors and black, gold and purple décor. The wait staff wore miniskirts, with midriff sexy tops revealing tan bare stomachs and of course, four inch heels. The DJ played current pop music by all the latest rock stars. They found a large table and sat down. Dallas ordered drinks for the table in the form of four bottles of extremely expensive wines.

Alli couldn't help scrutinizing the door for Sam. She really had her hopes up, but there was absolutely no guarantee he would show up. They were still eating when her group left, so it might be a bit before he arrived there.

The wine bottles were brought to the table and poured. Alli took a glass when Dallas handed it to her. It tasted extraordinarily good. Amazing how much better an expensive bottle of wine could taste versus the cheaper ones.

Finally, she saw Sam, Kevin, Tyler and Dustin walk in and sit at a table directly across the dance floor from her group.

"Well, I see he came," Susie remarked. "Now, don't you even think about going over there. You at least make him come to you."

"I will." Alli observed Sam's group order drinks. And it wasn't wine, not for Sam. No he would order a Jack Daniels Whiskey on the rocks.

Dallas engaged her in conversation again, by asking her questions about what she did, but she kept one eye on what Sam was doing. Then she saw him looking at her and she could have sworn he looked jealous.

The dance floor seemed to be filling up and then they played, *Single Ladies-Put A Ring On It*, by Beyoncé and suddenly the dance floor was full.

"Come on. Let's dance. This is your song," Kally said pulling Alli up off her chair and practically dragging her onto the dance floor.

Jennifer and Susie quickly followed.

This was one of her favorite songs, probably because of her situation with Sam. It had such a great beat that they couldn't help dancing and singing along. She looked over toward Sam's table and observed him watching her with somewhat of a frown on his face as he listened to the all too true words of the song.

Finally, the song ended and the music changed to a slow song by Prince of all people. Was this ironic or what? Being they were from Minnesota, and grew up in the 80's, they simply couldn't help being fans of Prince's music. The ultimate slow dance song, *When Dove's Cry*, began playing. They were walking off the dance floor when Alli suddenly felt strong male arms wrap around her waist and turn her around into a hard chest belonging to Sam.

"Can I have this dance?" Sam asked.

"Well since it's your birthday and all," Alli said.

Sam didn't need her to say anymore and pulled her even closer into his arms. They began slow dancing as their bodies moved in unison to the beat of the music.

Alli breathed in his Calvin Klein cologne and relaxed into the safe haven his arms provided her. She looked up into his dark brown eyes. These were the eyes she fell in love with and still loved. The urge to run her fingers through his lush jet black hair overwhelmed her, but she resisted. For now, anyway.

Sam pulled her tighter against him as if he would never let her go. Around and around they turned, moving slowly across the much less crowded dance floor. She could feel Susie, Kally and Jennifer's eyes boring into her back asking, 'What are you doing?' But it felt good. It felt right...exactly where she wanted to be. And not merely tonight but forever. Unfortunately, she had no idea what was going through his mind. She prayed he'd changed his mind, but she couldn't count on anything until he said he wanted to get back together. The song ended and she looked deeply into his searching eyes, trying to read his mind. Then, he kissed her. It was a long awaited reunion kiss and every inch of her body reacted passionately. Wanting him.

"We need to talk." He took her hand and led her to the door.

Alli followed him. Once outside the Oasis Club where the sound volume was much more tolerable, she said, "I need to go back in to grab my purse and sweater. Don't go anywhere. I'll be right back." She walked back into the Oasis Club and over to her table. Immediately, she observed Susie's eyes focus on her.

"You came back," Susie said.

"Basically to get my purse and sweater. I'm going to go someplace quiet to talk to him," Alli said.

"Tell me you're not going to his room," Susie stated.

"We are going to talk," Alli said.

"Right," Kally said. "Anyone who watched you two dancing, knows what he's thinking."

"Don't worry. Regardless, as you reminded me, 'What happens in Vegas, stays in Vegas,'" Alli stated calmly.

"Oh, my God! You're thinking about doing it!" Susie exclaimed.

"I don't know, we'll see what happens." Alli picked up her purse and sweater. "If I don't make it back to the room tonight, don't worry. I'll be fine."

"Are you sure about this?" Susie asked.

"I need to do this. I'll see you later or I'll call you in the morning." Alli hugged Susie, then quickly walked out to where she'd left Sam standing.

As soon as he saw her, his face lit up with a huge smile and he extended his hand to her. "Wasn't sure you'd be back."

"I've wanted to spend your 30th birthday with you for a long time. Didn't think it would happen, but I guess they don't call it *Lucky Vegas* for nothing. Let's go celebrate!" Alli flashed him a big smile that lit up her face, took his hand and they walked out of the casino's main entrance doors to catch a cab back to the main part of the strip.

CHAPTER 4

*A*lli and Sam got into the cab.

"Where to?" the cabbie asked.

"Bellagio," Sam answered.

Alli was unsure what to say so she said nothing but instead watched the bright lights of the Vegas hotels and casinos as they drove by. Sam was quiet, too. The conversation they needed to have did not need an audience, so waiting until they were in a more private place was for the best. Minutes later, the cab pulled up in front of the Bellagio.

They stepped out and Sam paid the cabbie. "Have you ever been to the Bellagio before?" He reached for her hand.

"No," Alli said.

"The water fountains show is supposed to be pretty cool. Let's walk over to watch it, I think it should be starting pretty soon."

Alli followed Sam to stand in front of the pools where the fountains were located. It was crowded, but they found a spot. Sam stood behind her with his arms wrapped around her waist. She felt safe in his arms. Always had. Minutes later, the music began playing and the fountains sprang to life. The music was techno orchestrated to have the multitude of fountains spray water up and down in various heights as if the water was dancing to the music.

Sam kissed her neck.

Alli felt the jolt of desire spread through her body, but she didn't turn around, even though she wanted nothing more than to kiss him at that moment.

He held her tightly against his body, as if to keep her from disappearing. "We talked about coming out here for a quick weekend getaway," Sam said.

"I know. We simply never seemed to find the time," Alli said.

"Odd, how fate took care of it for us."

"Almost like this was meant to be," Alli said.

"My sentiments exactly," Sam replied.

At that moment, the water fountains reached unbelievable heights and the lights flashed in red to the music. Alli was in awe. This would be a night she would always remember. And if it ended after a drink or two, it would still be a night she would never forget. They stood quietly watching the fabulous water, light and music display with their bodies pressed tightly against each other.

When the music ended, Alli turned around to face Sam. She could see the desire in his eyes, a look she knew all too well. He leaned down towards her and kissed her eagerly waiting lips. It was a long awaited and anticipated kiss. All the desire and love she felt for Sam came through in this soul searching heartfelt kiss.

"I've missed you," Sam said.

Alli welcomed the words with an open heart. "I've missed you too, Sam."

"Let's go have a drink inside. We need to talk." He took her hand and they walked into the Moulin Rouge cocktail bar.

They found a cozy little table by itself in the back corner. Taking a seat, Sam ordered a bottle of Beringer White Zinfandel wine. He obviously remembered it was her favorite. On the stage in the far opposite corner, a small band played slow blues songs with a quite talented female lead singer who had the crooning blues style down to a tee.

They listened and seconds later, the waitress was pouring wine in their glasses.

"Alli, I'm sorry I didn't call," Sam said.

"I was waiting for you to call," she said.

"I wanted to. I can't tell you how many times I picked up the phone to call you but didn't."

"Why didn't you?" she asked.

Sam took her hands in his and looked into her eyes. "It's not because I didn't love you. You know that I do, don't you?"

"I thought so, but when you never called, I convinced myself that you didn't," Alli said.

"It was never that. You know that. I was just plain scared."

"Scared? Of what?"

"The responsibility that goes along with being married and having a family."

"Did you think it didn't scare me, too? But we were in it together and I knew we would figure it out," Alli said.

"For a guy it's different."

"How? That's the part I never understood," Alli asked.

"It's a huge commitment financially."

"We were already living together, what would've been different?"

"What if it didn't work out? If you're not married, it's easier to walk away. Come on, Alli, we both have friends who went through divorces. And it got downright nasty. Plus, it cost a lot."

"So it was all about money?" Alli asked.

"No, not so much the money. But people change. What if we wake up one day and don't like each other anymore?"

"That is what the commitment part of marriage is all about. You try to work it out and fix what went wrong. You have to rely on the love we have for each other to get us through the bad times, if there are any."

"I love you, that was never in question," Sam said.

Alli felt relief wash over her. He said he loved her. There was a chance for them still then. "I never stopped loving you, Sam."

He had been squeezing her hand tightly, then his grip relaxed and loosened. "I'm sorry I was so stubborn. I should've called you."

"Sam, what about the other part?" Alli asked.

"What part?" Sam asked.

"Having children."

"I'm not against ever having children. They just totally scare the hell out of me," Sam said.

"Why? You like kids. I've seen you with your nephews and nieces and you are great," Alli offered.

"I like kids. Never said I didn't. But taking care of them on a full time basis is a whole other story."

"You wouldn't be doing it alone, we'd be doing it together. It's not that tough," Alli said.

"Having a kid is an even bigger commitment," Sam said.

"The actual giving birth, scares the heck out of me but it will be worth it to hold our child in my arms. Children can bring a lot of joy to our lives, too. But, they can be a lot of work."

"I don't know anything about raising kids," Sam said.

"I don't think anyone does when they first start out, but they figure it out thanks to friends, families, expert advice in books and on the internet."

"Couldn't we wait a while on having a baby?" Sam asked. "One thing at a time."

"Sam, I'm thirty and my biological clock is ticking. I can't wait or I might not be able to have a baby down the line. I know it's different for guys. You can have a baby till you're eighty. Women can't." She could see him thinking and weighing the odds on what he wanted and what he didn't want, at least right now. She could only hope he wanted her bad enough to have a baby soon enough."

The song playing was slow and there were people dancing.

He stood up and reached for her hand, "Let's dance."

Alli got up knowing he was done talking about getting married and having a baby. At least, for now. She moved closer to him, wrapping her arms around his strong back and placing her head on his chest. She could hear his heart beating. He was a good man and she loved him more than she had ever loved anyone. She couldn't imagine spending her life without him. The past six months had been pure hell. In his arms was where she wanted to be. Hopefully, he would come around and take the chance.

They danced and relished touching each other's bodies. After the dance, he kissed her again. Back at the table, they changed the subject to talking about what had been going on at their work offices. Her job as the Office Manager at Oak Tree Medical had been basically uneventful. His job as a Financial Planner at his parents' company, Cavera Financial, had its ups and downs with the volatile economy. The wine bottle ran empty and another appeared as they talked. Her glass was always full so she kept sipping it while they talked about everything and everyone, trying to catch each other up on the last six months. Another bottle became empty and a new one appeared. Alli was feeling the effects of the wine, so she slowed down her sips as she watched Sam empty the bottle.

It was hard to keep track of time since Vegas never shuts down, but she felt sure it was at least two o'clock in the morning. Sam paid the check and she held onto his arm as they walked out together. Alli was having a hard time concentrating at this point. She'd drank way more than she was used to. When they walked out the main doors of the Bellagio, they got into a cab. Alli assumed they would be going to his hotel room. She would be okay with anywhere they could be alone. She loved Sam and wanted to feel his naked body against her naked body while they made love. And the sooner the better.

CHAPTER 5

"*W*here to sir?" asked the cab driver.

The bellman opened the door for Alli and she stepped in.

Still standing outside the open door, Sam said, "The nicest Wedding Chapel on the Strip."

The cab driver frowned. "You sure, Man? It looks like you've had a lot to drink."

"Never been more sure." Sam got into the backseat of the cab and pulled Alli close to him.

A few minutes later, the cab pulled up in front of the Desert Chapel. The cab driver got out and opened the door for them to get out. Alli got out with Sam close behind her. He immediately pulled her close and kissed her again.

Alli looked at the sign that read, "Weddings 24 HOURS."

"You've talked me into it. Let's do it," Sam said and they walked into the chapel.

"Getting married?" the woman at the desk asked.

"Yes," Sam answered.

"Both of you sure this is what you want? This is the real thing. It's a legal marriage." The woman smiled.

"Positive," Sam said.

"Yes," Alli said. "I've waited a long time to do this."

"Do you want the Deluxe Package?" the woman asked.

"Yes, the best," Sam said.

The woman at the desk, took their ID's, filled out the forms, and told them where to sign. Sam signed. Alli signed. She led them into the chapel where the Justice of the Peace stood ready to perform the ceremony. The room had six church benches on each side with a center aisle. The woman disappeared then reappeared with a veil and a bouquet of white roses. Music played in the background. Some song about love. Alli couldn't quite recall which one it was. She stood in the front of the chapel with Sam and the Justice of the Peace stood in front of them in a black suit.

He read the marriage vows consisting of the usual lines. "...to honor and obey. Do you take this woman to be your lawfully wedded wife? Then answer I do."

"Yes, I do," Sam said.

The man repeated and asked, "Do you take this man to be your lawfully wedded husband? Then answer I do."

"Yes, I do," Alli said.

"I now pronounce you man and wife. You may kiss the bride," the Justice of the Peace announced.

Sam took Alli in his arms and kissed her.

"I love you, Alli."

"I love you, Sam."

They followed the woman out of the chapel to the front desk where she stamped some documents and the Justice of the Peace signed them.

She handed Sam two copies. "Congratulations," she said.

"Thank you." Sam folded the copies and put them in his pants pocket.

The cab was still waiting outside for them. "Where to?" the cab driver asked.

"The Palms."

Minutes later, the cab arrived at The Palms Hotel. They stepped out, Sam paid the cabbie, and they walked into the hotel's main lobby entrance. Once inside, they made their way to the elevators. It stopped on the 12th floor which was where Sam's room was located. He slid the key card in and they entered the room.

Thank God, he had booked his own separate room. He turned on the light and shut the door behind them. There were no holds barred now. He kissed Alli and his hands freely roamed her body. A body he knew all too well. He found the zipper and unzipped the dress while he continued kissing her. He could feel her hands on his chest unbuttoning his shirt. He almost lost it when her hands touched his bare chest. Her dress slid forward and she slid her arms out so it could slide to the floor. He pulled his shirt off and gazed at the beautiful woman standing in front of him wearing a sexy revealing bra that laid her breasts out on display along with a tiny thong panty. She still had on her four inch black heels. He was certain a man couldn't ask for anything more than what stood provocatively in front of him. He reached in for a taut breast that filled his hand. They were backed up to the bed, so he laid her down on it visually taking in all of her while he unzipped his pants and dropped them to the floor. He kicked off his shoes and kneeled over her on the bed.

"I love you," he said. His lips found her nipple quickly and he felt her body arch beneath his. He was ready and hard. God, it had been a long time. He kissed her while he unhooked the bra and dropped it to the floor.

Alli pulled the thong off and it too, dropped to the floor along with the high heels. She straddled him and teased him with her breasts until his mouth found them one by one, while she rubbed her wet opening against his hardness. She leaned in close to kiss him. "I love you, Sam."

He couldn't wait any longer. He rolled on top of her, seeking entrance, pushing slowly at first, then further while picking up speed until they both were writhing. Alli cried out her pleasure and then he immediately allowed his seed to spill inside of her.

Sam rolled to her side, pulling her onto his chest.

"That was wonderful. I've missed you," she said.

"I've missed you," Sam said. Alli was his and he wasn't letting her go this time. They'd always had great sex. She was so damn beautiful. He loved her and she loved him. What more could he ask for?

Minutes later, they both were asleep.

CHAPTER 6

*S*am woke to his phone vibrating. He'd slept lightly, waking a few times to make sure Alli was still in his arms. Right now, all he knew was his head hurt something fierce. It never was a good thing to mix hard liquor, namely Jack Daniels Whiskey with wine. He vaguely remembered the previous night except for the great sex. Of course, it had always been that way with them.

The question was why was his phone vibrating with a beeping noise, which meant it wasn't a call? Damn! It was six o'clock. His flight was leaving at eight o'clock that morning. The guys had tried to talk him out of leaving so early, but there was a golf event for his company and although he didn't have to golf in it, he needed to be at the dinner after golfing. Unfortunately, since they had booked the trip only a couple of weeks ago, the only flight he could get back was a connecting flight in Denver, with a Vegas departure time at eight.

He looked over at Alli. She was sound asleep. He knew she had drunk way more than she was used to and probably needed to sleep it off. He got up and went in the bathroom to take a quick shower. After he was done, he checked and she was still asleep. He dressed quickly in jeans and threw his stuff in his bag. He picked up his black dress pants from last night to fold into the suitcase. First, he checked the pockets and pulled out some folded papers. He went to throw them in the garbage, but unfolded them first to see what they were.

Sam couldn't believe what he saw. State of Nevada Marriage License. It looked very official and had his and Alli's names on it with a very official looking seal. There were two copies and a receipt from the Desert Wedding Chapel. He looked over at Alli. *What had they done last night? Shit!* He knew he'd drank too much, but enough to go and get married? When he looked at her though all he felt was love for her. Hell, it could've been worse. He could've gone and married a perfect stranger. But no, it had been Alli who he loved dearly. Would she even remember? Hell, he didn't remember. He picked up the receipt to read it more carefully. The ceremony was filmed and he could order a copy of it on a DVD to be mailed to his address. Great. Well then, he would know if it was real or not. But hell, his gut told him it was real. He could totally feel it. The way he'd felt yesterday about finally seeing her again after six months, he knew it was definitely something he would've done. He put the pants in the suitcase and closed it. The receipt and marriage license he folded back up and put in his wallet. He'd deal with this when they were both back in Minneapolis. Hell, he hadn't even asked her how long she was staying in Vegas.

Alli turned over in the bed, but didn't wake up.

He looked around the room to make sure he had everything. He vaguely remembered a bouquet of roses but it wasn't in the room. She must've left it at the chapel or in the cab. The hotel checkout receipt was lying on the floor by the door. He picked it up. He'd given the hotel his card when he checked in so everything was already paid.

He looked at the time on his phone and realized he had to go. He walked over to the bed and touched Alli's cheek. "Alli," he said.

"Sam," she answered trying to focus on him.

"I have an early flight back to Minneapolis this morning. I have to go. The room is paid for. I always get a late check out, so you don't have to be out till one o'clock, so go back to sleep."

"Do you have to leave?" she asked.

"I have a work event I need to be at tonight. Sorry. Wish I could stay," he said brushing the hair from her face.

"I love you, Sam."

"I love you, too. When will you be back?" he asked.

"Monday late."

"I'll call you Tuesday." Sam kissed her and left.

He knew he was being a coward. He should've merely called his dad and told him he couldn't make it back, and stayed with Alli to figure out what they'd done and what they were going to do going forward. All he knew was he needed to get back and he needed some time to figure things out.

Sam caught a cab to the airport and arrived with only thirty minutes to spare. He texted the guys and told them he was on his way back to Minneapolis. For only a moment, he wondered what he would do if she didn't remember at all. He could absolutely have the marriage annulled or whatever you did under those extenuating circumstances. But did he want that? He wanted Alli. He knew that much. It was just the whole marriage thing he felt unsure about. A part of him felt bad though because he knew Alli always wanted the big church wedding. He didn't want to jip her out of her dream wedding, either. And truth be told, if he took the big step and got married, he wanted the big church wedding, too. The one they had always talked about, only in his mind it was much further down the line than what Alli had anticipated.

It all depended on whether Alli remembered the marriage. If she didn't, he could simply let it go, then they could go ahead and plan the big wedding. Even if she remembered, they could just not tell anyone else about it and go ahead with her wedding plans. Who would know besides them and the Vegas Chapel? That was his plan and it would work. He would just have to wait until Tuesday to talk to her.

He remembered last night and her lying naked in his bed this morning, and he knew when he saw her on Tuesday, he would be spending the night with her at either her place or his. After all, she was now his wife. Even if she didn't remember.

Sam boarded the plane.

∽

ALLI WOKE up about ten to an empty bed. She remembered Sam making love to her last night. It had felt so good, but then with Sam it always was great. Where was he? She sat up in the bed. This was his hotel room, but he was gone. Her head hurt something fierce. She had drunk way more wine than she was accustomed to, that was for sure. She got up and made her way to the bathroom. What she really needed was some Tylenol, but she knew there wasn't any in her small evening purse.

Where was Sam? She vaguely remembered him sitting on the side of the bed this morning fully dressed. What had he said? Something about an early flight? Hell, he'd left her here alone. She didn't have any clothes to change into or any of her toiletries or makeup. Now what should she do? Her phone, where was her phone?

She found her purse, reached inside and pulled her phone out. She saw Susie had texted her already this morning. She texted back saying she was in Sam's room at The Palms Hotel and to bring her makeup and clothes to Sam's hotel room. Hell, she didn't know what room she was in. She walked over to the room phone on the desk to check the room number—1212. She finished the text to Susie and waited for a reply.

Minutes later, a text beeped in from Susie—I'm on my way.

Alli walked into the bathroom and stepped into the shower. After she was done, she wrapped the towel around her then went to sit on the bed and wait for Susie to bring her stuff.

While she waited, she tried desperately to remember what Sam said before he left. Something about a work event, he had to be at tonight, but what else? He said he'd call, that was it. But when? Tuesday kept popping into her head. Yes, he would call her Tuesday after she got back to Minneapolis. She definitely remembered him telling her he loved her. That was good. She would go with that until Tuesday.

She heard a knock at the door.

"Alli," Susie called out.

Alli walked to the door and opened it to let Susie into the room. Alli hugged her. "Thank you for bringing my stuff. You're the best."

"I know and don't you forget it." Susie looked around the room. "Where is Sam? Looks like his stuff is gone."

"He had an early flight, so he had to leave. We drank a few bottles of wine before we got to his room." Alli opened the her toiletry bag, took out the bottle of Tylenol, opened it, dropped two into her mouth then took a big drink of water from the bottle on the desk.

"Your head hurt?" Susie asked.

"Maybe a little bit," Alli said, holding two fingers up to show a little bit.

"So what happened last night? I'm assuming from the looks of things here, you slept with him."

"Yes. It was fabulous," Alli said and walked into the bathroom with her bag and make up. She began combing her hair, then drying it.

"But he left."

"He's going to call me on Tuesday when I get back."

"And then what? The two of you will live happily ever after?" Susie asked.

"Don't be so sarcastic. You know we are good together and we love each other. It'll be all right."

"So now, you don't care about getting married and having a baby?" Susie asked.

"Of course, I still care. We talked about getting married and having a baby last night," Alli said.

"And he agreed to both?" Susie asked in shock.

"Not exactly, but he didn't say no either," Alli said.

"So you are right back where you started from."

"No, I think he's going to be okay with it now," Alli said.

"And what makes you think that? Simply because he slept with you?" Susie asked.

"He missed me and he loves me." Alli put her clothes on, jeans and a tank top with a fitted hoodie jacket.

"Okay, whatever. Are you at least going to try and have some fun while you're out here for the rest of the trip?" Susie asked.

"Of course. Just not looking for a man, now." Alli folded up her dress and put it in her bag along with her high heels. She finished drying her hair then put the toiletry and make-up bag back inside her bag.

"I hope you know what you're doing," Susie said.

"He is the love of my life. You know that." Alli looked around the room to make sure she had everything and they left.

On the elevator ride down, Alli reached in her purse and pulled out a twenty dollar bill.

"What's that for?" Susie asked.

"I'm feeling lucky today. I'm going to find a slot machine that speaks to me, play my twenty dollars and see what happens."

"Now, you're talking my language." Susie laughed.

They exited the elevator and walked into the casino game floor. They wandered down a couple of aisles when Alli spotted a slot machine with rings on it. Engagement rings with lots of bling. "This is it."

"*Put A Ring On It?*" Susie laughed.

"Yes. Either was that song or *Holding out for a Hero*!" Alli sat down in front of the machine and put her twenty dollars in the slot. On the third spin, she hit five matching rings. The lights went off and believe it or not, Beyoncé's song played.

Susie was sitting at the machine behind Alli's and turned around. "I don't believe it. You just won a thousand dollars!"

"Really? I told you I felt lucky today," Alli said and pressed the cash out button.

"Aren't you going to play anymore?" Susie asked.

"Nope. My motto is take the money and run!" Alli said. The machine printed out a slip. "Yes! I finally hit a jackpot."

Susie finished up her twenty without winning anything and they walked over to the cashier's window to cash out Alli's ticket.

The cashier counted out ten one hundred dollar bills for her.

Alli put the money in her wallet. She couldn't help smiling. This was definitely her lucky day! And in more ways than one.

CHAPTER 7

*A*lli and the girls spent the rest of their Vegas trip at the pool every afternoon with all the hot convention men, then went to dinner, shows and clubs in the evening. Kally, Susie and Jennifer were looking for men who interested them, but Alli was only along for the ride. She couldn't even think about other men when all she could think about was Sam.

At the pool, the girls relaxed in their chaise lounges taking in the sun while reading romance novels with happy endings, which was what they were all looking for.

"Alli!" Susie called to her.

"What? What's wrong?" Alli asked.

"Billy. Did you forget about him?" Susie asked.

"Yeah, he's such a nice guy. I thought you liked him?" Kally added.

"We're only friends," Alli said.

"Does he know that?" Jennifer asked. "I think he likes you more than friends."

"I can't help that. I told him I simply wanted to be friends."

"Why? Don't you think he's hot? I think he's hot," Kally said.

"He's not bad looking. There just simply isn't any chemistry there." Alli made a sad face.

"That's because you're still hot for Sam," Jennifer said.

"I think Billy is merely waiting for you to get over Sam," Kally stated.

"He's going to be waiting a long time for that," Susie interjected.

"Let's face it," Alli added. "Even if Sam wasn't in the picture, I'm totally not interested in Billy that way."

"Can I have him then?" Kally said.

"Don't let me hold you back," Alli said.

"Hey, isn't that Dallas over there? I think he's interested in you Alli. What do you think of him? Any chemistry?" Jennifer asked.

"He intrigues me a little and he's nice enough. But..." Alli observed Dallas walk towards them.

"Hi ladies," Dallas said as he walked directly over to Alli's chair where he stopped. "Would you ladies like to join us tonight for dinner at the Wynn and the show, *Le Reve?*"

Sebastian, Troy and Trevor joined him as they surveyed the tan sexy bodies laid out on the chairs.

"We'd love to." Kally couldn't help smiling at Sebastian.

"Great. We'll meet you in the lobby at six." Dallas smiled at Alli and the four men walked back into the casino.

"What did you just get us into?" Alli asked Kally.

"Don't get all hot and bothered. It's only dinner and a show. You don't have to sleep with him," Kally said.

"I don't intend to," Alli said.

"I do," Kally said smiling.

"Me, too," Jennifer said.

"Whatever. You guys can totally do whatever you want," Alli said. "Maybe I shouldn't go. That way, Dallas won't get his hopes up."

"You're going," Kally stated. "There's four guys and there needs to be four girls. You have to eat anyway and besides, you are the one who wanted to see, *Le Reve.*"

"Okay. I have heard that show is fabulous," Alli said.

~

AT SIX, the four ladies walked into the lobby dressed in their newly purchased dresses from the outlet mall just a few blocks away only a few hours ago. The fashionistas were tan, trim and fit causing many heads to turn their way as they walked through the casino floor occupied by mostly men from the convention.

Dallas, Sebastian, Trevor and Troy were casually waiting for their dinner dates and witnessed their approach with sincere appreciation for their beauty, along with being thankful that they could be the lucky men who were spending the evening with these four hot sexy women.

Each man took a lady's arm. Dallas, Alli's arm. Sebastian, Kally's arm. Trevor, Susie's arm. And Troy, Jennifer's arm. The four couples walked out the doors and into a waiting limo. Twenty minutes later, they arrived at the Wynn, which was one of the most expensive hotels on the Vegas strip and the most elaborate. No expense had been spared in its design, both inside and outside.

The guys made reservations at the Wynn Elite for dinner and they were immediately escorted to a table upon arrival. Alli watched her friends having the time of their lives with these men. Unfortunately, they would probably never see them again after tomorrow. She was somewhat drawn in by Dallas' charm, but she knew he would never compare to her Sam. And Sam would be in Minneapolis waiting for her on Tuesday. Wouldn't he? He'd made no guarantees except that he would call her. Oh, and that he did love her. But she knew all that before they broke up six months ago. What had changed? Nothing, really. They'd had fabulous sex but what would that change? She needed to see it through and give Sam the benefit of the doubt.

Dallas was nice though, and she knew she was attracted to him. So she decided to play it safe and try to give him a chance for now, anyway. She wasn't going to sleep with him but that didn't mean she couldn't flirt a little and have a good time. Just in case things didn't work out with Sam, she intended to leave this door open.

Dinner was delicious. Of course, it was the Wynn and you could expect nothing less. After dinner, they walked to the other end of the hotel for the show, stopping along the way to gaze at the beautiful items of clothing available to purchase for a small fortune. These were items she and her friends could never afford, but the men seemed unaffected by the prices. She had an odd feeling the guys came from money. In fact, probably all their families had money.

The show was sold out and there was definitely a full house. She was expecting a lot from the show, considering all the reviews she'd read stated no one in the audience had been disappointed.

Le Reve met all her expectations and the cast was unbelievably talented.

Afterwards, they took the limo to the Hard Rock Club to go dancing. The club was crowded but the guys had reserved a table in the VIP section, so they were seated immediately. The whole group hit the dance floor. Alli danced with Dallas. Many drinks were ordered. Although, Alli only had a couple of glasses of wine. Unlike last night, she intended to remember everything that happened this evening. About one in the morning, the limo finally headed back to their hotel.

Alli felt sufficiently confident that all the men were going to get lucky tonight except for Dallas. The three other couples went off to their hotel rooms and she was left standing alone in the lobby with Dallas.

"I take it you're not up to inviting me to your room," he stated cautiously.

"I'm sorry, but I don't do one night stands," Alli said putting it out there straight forward, so he wouldn't be disappointed.

"I understand. I wouldn't want you to feel pressured."

"Good. I need to get to know someone for a while before I jump into bed with them. And we will probably never see each other again, after tonight."

"I would like to get your number to call you. I know long distance relationships are difficult, but for you I'd give it a shot. You're one special lady," he said. "Can I at least walk you to your room?"

Alli nodded. What else could she do at this point? They walked to the elevators and stepped inside. She hit floor seven and the elevator doors closed.

They arrived on her floor and walked to room 712. Alli got

nervous at this point, realizing she was alone with him. "I'm glad we got to meet each other. You're a great guy and I had a nice time," Alli said.

Dallas leaned towards her and kissed her. It wasn't like Sam's kisses, but it wasn't bad either, she thought. He ended the kiss and smiled.

He reached into his pocket and handed her his business card. "Call me if you change your mind later and want to give a long distance relationship a chance. Cuz, I'm definitely interested." Dallas turned and walked back down the hall toward the elevator.

Alli reached into her purse for her room key card, opened the door and stepped into her room. She pulled out her billfold and put his card inside. Just in case it didn't work out with Sam, she told herself.

CHAPTER 8

Seated on the plane from Vegas to Minneapolis, next to Susie, Alli couldn't stop thinking about Sam. It had only been two days but it seemed like such a long time ago that they'd spent the night together making love once again. A big part of her was very afraid to think that they wouldn't be getting back together. Or worse yet, what if they tried but he still couldn't commit and wouldn't marry her? Again. She wasn't sure she could survive another break up. Why were all her thoughts negative when it came to their relationship? The big question was, what happened if he didn't call? This was her last thought before she fell asleep with her head leaning on the window.

Alli woke to the flight attendant's announcement stating they would be landing shortly. She stared out the window at the Twin Cities sprawled out below them in neat little squares filled with houses and businesses. Somewhere down there, Sam was going on about his life. One question kept nagging in the back of her mind. *Is he thinking about me?*

They deplaned and walked to the baggage area. Alli remained silent.

"Alli, you're awful quiet. You okay?" Susie asked.

"Yes."

"Who are you thinking about? Sam? Dallas? Billy?" Susie asked.

"Very funny," Alli said.

"You didn't answer," Susie countered.

"Sam."

"Figures," Susie said as they watched the suitcases going by on the carousel.

Alli spotted her suitcase and grabbed it.

Susie spotted hers and minutes later, they were walking out to Susie's car in the parking ramp.

"You know he may not call at all," Susie stated.

"That's always a possibility. He'll call though," Alli said.

Shortly after Susie dropped her off, her phone rang. Alli ran across the room to grab her phone out of her purse. She saw Billy's name on the caller ID. She debated on whether to answer. Even though she really didn't want to, she knew he would totally keep calling to see if she'd made it home and how the trip was. "Hello," she said as she swiped the screen.

"Alli, you're back. Just wanted to see how your trip was. Fun, I hope," Billy said.

"Vegas was Vegas. We sat at the pool, ate, shopped and saw a show. Oh and I won $1,000."

"Congratulations. Do you want to get together this week and you can tell me all about it?" he asked.

"Not sure what my plans are yet," Alli said.

"Okay, I'll check back in a couple of days. You're probably tired from traveling. I'll let you go."

"It has been a long day. Talk to you later," she said and hung up.

Alli walked over to her couch and collapsed on it. Sam had said Tuesday and it was only Monday. She had to go to work in the morning, so she needed to unpack and get ready for her week. And she definitely needed to stop thinking about Sam. If he called, he called and if didn't, then life would go on just like it had before.

Regardless, she really needed to have a serious talk with Billy. If he was waiting for her to get over Sam, he would be waiting a long time because she wasn't interested in him that way. She needed to make that clear. It wasn't fair to lead him on. Sadly though, he was a good friend and she did enjoy his company. It sure beat the heck out of doing everything by herself. Well or with Susie. Susie may be busy in the future, trying out her new long term relationship with Trevor, which would certainly involve very long phone calls, and probably multiple calls a day.

SAM MADE it back to Minneapolis and attended the event for work. Monday at the office, he kept thinking about Alli and wondering what she'd been doing in Vegas. What kept nagging at him was the guy she'd been having dinner with at the Palms. He'd seen the way the guy looked at Alli which definitely showed his interest in her. And now since he was back in Minneapolis, this guy had her all to himself. It made him absolutely furious.

He checked his messages and saw a text from Tori. He'd gone out with her once a few weeks ago after concluding he and Alli were really over and he needed to move on. Mainly, because Alli hadn't called even once in six months. Never mind that he hadn't bothered to call her, either. Tori was attractive and fun, but she definitely wasn't Alli. He texted her back, stating he had a very busy week. Right now, he wasn't even the least bit interested in seeing her.

Tuesday all day, he tried to figure out what he should say about the marriage certificate. Hell, they were married. Something he'd fought for the past six and a half years. Now it was done and he wasn't sure what to do. If he was going to be married, he certainly wanted to enjoy the benefits, that was for sure. He wanted Alli in his bed every night like before. He'd grown accustomed to her being there and when she wasn't, he missed her.

Tuesday afternoon, he sent Alli a text asking her to meet him after work for a drink at *BonFire*. He would wait and see if she said anything about the wedding chapel. Then he would figure out how to proceed.

~

AT SIX O'CLOCK, Alli waited in the lobby for Sam. She observed his car pull into the parking lot and waited patiently for him to walk through the front door. He smiled when he saw her. She stood up as he walked over and kissed her on the lips. Exactly the way he used to do when they were together. This could be a good sign.

"How was your day?" he asked taking in her smile.

"Good, how about you?" she asked.

The hostess led them to a table where they ordered drinks and appetizers.

"We need to talk about what happened," Sam said.

"I know," she said.

"It was really an odd twist of fate that we were both in Vegas at the same time."

"Do you think we can try it again?" Alli asked.

"I've really missed you," Sam said. "I've missed waking up every morning to you lying next to me in bed."

"Me, too," Alli said.

"So where do we go from here?"

"Do you think you can make the commitments I need in the very near future?" she asked.

"I think we are much closer to that than we were before," he answered.

"I can't simply move back in. Maybe we should just start dating again, and see how it goes," Alli suggested.

"Does that include spending the night?" he asked.

"Possibly," she said. "But we need to move towards setting a wedding date."

"Woah, can we go out on a few dates first," he said laughing.

"Okay, that is a perfectly legitimate request." Alli laughed.

"Alli, would you like to go out on Saturday night?" he asked.

"I'd love to." She smiled while her heart pounded in her chest as she pictured her and Sam naked in his bed. "What do you want to do?"

"Let me check out what's going on in town and then we can decide."

Their appetizers and drinks were placed on the table in front of them. The conversation was light. They laughed. They talked. They drank.

A couple of hours later, they walked to their cars. Sam took her in his arms and kissed her. "I don't know. Saturday seems a long ways away. Maybe we should make it Friday."

"Friday works for me. But I have one request," Alli said.

"What is it?"

"I'll give you six months and if by the end of the six months, you aren't ready to set a wedding date, we call it quits, for good."

"Deal. But, I don't think I can wait until Friday night, how about Thursday night?" he asked.

Alli was ecstatic. His desire for her was extremely evident and nothing made her happier. "Thursday it is," she stated.

Alli got in her car as Sam walked to his car.

CHAPTER 9

"He called," Alli said into her phone.

"Not really any surprise. He definitely wants to get you into bed again," Susie said.

"Is that so bad? We always have great sex."

"No, but you want more and he doesn't want to give you more. Or has he changed his mind?" Susie asked.

"We're going to give it six months and if we can't set a wedding date by then, we're done for good."

"Okay. But what makes you think this time will be different?" Susie asked.

"He said we were a lot closer to him making a commitment than we ever were before. In fact, it still sounded like he was more afraid of having kids than getting married."

"Right. I never thought he didn't want to marry you, it's always been about having kids."

"I think he's just plain scared of the unknown," Alli said.

"And exactly how is six months going to change his mind about kids?" Susie asked.

"I don't know, but I'm going to try my darndest to bring him around to being okay with becoming a family man."

"Sam's a nice guy, don't get me wrong. You know we all like him, but you have a tough job ahead of you. But, who knows maybe this break up you guys had will have been enough to knock some sense into his thick skull. For your sake, I hope so."

"We're going to start out slow. Start dating again and go from there."

"Good! I was afraid you were going to just move back in with him right away."

"No. I'm definitely not going to do that. If it doesn't work out, I want to still have my own place. I'm not moving back into his place unless I have an engagement ring and wedding date."

"Glad to see you have a plan. So when's the next date?"

"Thursday night."

"Wow, not wasting any time are you! Couldn't wait till the weekend?"

"Saturday was just too far away. And so was Friday."

"I guess tomorrow was too soon, so you only had Thursday left." Susie laughed.

"You got it!"

"Trevor called me tonight, in case you were wondering."

"That's great! Right? I mean you wanted him to call, right?"

"I guess so. I just don't know how people do these long distance relationships. It sucks to know you can't see each other for who knows how long."

"Chicago, isn't that far away."

"I know, but it's not merely across town either. He's going to come to see me in a couple of weeks."

"Susie, don't say anything about me and Sam to him. I'll tell Dallas after I see how it's going with Sam. Okay?"

"Sure. That's a girl. Keep those options open, just in case. Listen, gotta get going. I'll talk to you later," Susie said and disconnected the call.

What was she thinking? Keeping her options open? She didn't want to even think about it not working out with Sam, but if it didn't, it would sure be nice to have someone else to fall back on. Dallas was

a great guy and if she hadn't run into Sam in Vegas, she would seri-
ously be thinking about trying a long distance relationship. Colorado
was a nice place and she wouldn't mind living in Denver. Unfortunately, Dallas had already left her a voicemail asking if she made it
back to Minneapolis all right. There was no way she was going to be
able to keep him hanging on for six months. Absolutely wasn't going
to happen. Probably telling him the truth would be the best thing to
do. It would just really suck though. Probably wouldn't hurt to give
her and Sam a couple of weeks first though.

Alli spent the next two days thinking about Sam and their date on
Thursday night. He'd emailed her to meet him at Brunswick Lanes in
Burnsville and they'd go bowling. She hadn't been there yet since it
just opened last summer. They were both good bowlers and had been
on bowling league teams in the past. She bowled in a women's league
and he bowled in a men's league. They'd been on their teams for years
and never felt they wanted to devote another night for bowling to
bowl on a couple's league. The new bowling alley was supposed to be
top of the line with all the latest gadgets, including a restaurant that
actually served tasty food and the latest fashionable bar drinks.

She sent him a reply and looked forward to seeing Sam.

She also sent Dallas an email saying she arrived safely back to
Minneapolis and was back to work. There were no details included
about what she had going on in her life. She thanked him for the nice
time in Vegas and let him know how much she enjoyed the Le Reve
show at the Wynn.

After work on Thursday, she rushed home to change clothes for
her date with Sam. Her new jeans with rhinestones on the back
pockets that fit her like a glove would do the trick. A low-cut, tight-
fitting black top would go well with them. She quickly touched up her
make-up and hair. The diamond necklace, Sam gave her for
Christmas last year looked perfect with the shirt. She didn't wear it
too often, because it reminded her of the break up. Plus, everyone
knew it was from Sam. When she opened her Christmas present from
Sam on Christmas Eve, she'd been positive it was the engagement ring
she'd been waiting over six years to receive. It was a small jeweler's

box, exactly the right size. When she saw the necklace in the box instead of the ring, her heart had broken into a million pieces. It said what he obviously couldn't say to her face. He didn't want to marry her. When she looked up, she realized he didn't even realize what he'd just done. The diamond necklace was beautiful. The diamond was big. But it wasn't in a ring. A tear had slid down her cheek. Sam thought it was because she was happy. But that hadn't been the reason. She had smiled then and asked him to help her put it on. After all, it was Christmas Eve. And that wasn't the proper time to tell him how he'd broken her heart that night.

It took a couple of weeks before she found the courage to talk to him about what the future held for them. He actually appeared to be surprised by her revelation. If they weren't getting engaged and getting married, they were done. Unfortunately for both of them, he hadn't thought she was serious about moving out. But the following Saturday, she borrowed her friend's pick-up truck and moved her stuff out. Sam hadn't even realized that all her friends thought they were getting engaged at Christmas, too. Everyone assumed it, except for Sam.

So why was she going to wear it tonight? She wasn't so sure it was the right thing to do either, but she wanted to remind him that he'd given her the necklace instead of an engagement ring. It was a huge obstacle in their relationship. One that needed to be rectified in less than six months or there would not be a 'Sam and Alli' anymore.

Alli made it to the bowling alley at seven sharp. She walked in and found Sam waiting in the restaurant. He had a table and smiled as she walked towards him. She could tell he liked what he was looking at by the way his eyes glazed over.

"You look great, Babe," Sam said as he stood up to embrace her.

"Thanks," Alli said right before his lips gently brushed her lips in a tease of more to come.

"Hope you're hungry. I've heard they have great food here." He handed her a menu as his eyes roved to her cleavage and the diamond pendant nestled perfectly above it.

Alli watched his eyes as they lowered to her cleavage, knowing he couldn't miss the necklace.

He hesitated a moment while fixated on it, but said nothing. Instead, he proceeded to read over the menu.

The waiter came over, took their order, and returned shortly with a beer for Sam and a glass of wine for Alli.

They ate and shared outstanding bowling scores they'd bowled recently. Afterwards, they walked to their lane carrying their own bowling balls and shoes.

"Want to place a wager on who bowls the highest score?" Sam asked.

"Sure. What will I win?" Alli asked.

"Pretty confident aren't you," Sam said as he walked up to her and pulled her into his arms against his rock hard chest.

"Damn straight! You know I'm going to kick your ass!" she exclaimed.

"Whoever wins gets to decide when and where our next date is," Sam said smiling.

"Okay, you're on," Alli said and walked over to the alley. She picked up her ball and threw a strike.

Sam cheered, "Way to go!" He walked over, picked up his ball, and threw a strike.

"Well, we both knew this was an even match."

Alli and Sam's scores were tied until the tenth frame, where Alli left 1 pin standing. Sam bowled a perfect 300 and won.

Alli walked over and kissed him. "Guess you won."

"Tomorrow night at my place. I'll make dinner."

"What time should I be there?" she asked.

"Seven."

"I'm looking forward to dinner," she said smiling. "Any thoughts on what you want to do after dinner?"

"Let's just see what we can come up with," Sam said as they walked to their cars.

They stopped at Alli's car. Sam turned Alli around and pressed her body against him as his lips devoured hers. Their hearts were pounding rapidly when he broke the embrace.

"Till tomorrow," he said and walked off towards his car.

Alli got in her car. She looked upward and prayed, "Please God, let this work out for us. If he breaks my heart again, I don't know if I will ever get over it this time."

CHAPTER 10

Sam left work early so he could stop by the meat market to pick up a couple of fresh cut porterhouse steaks, Idaho baking potatoes and brussel sprouts. For dessert, he picked up fresh made, always delicious, fresh strawberry cheesecake from the Cheesecake Factory. Then the liquor store for a bottle of Beringer White Zinfandel. Her favorite. He wanted dinner to be perfect.

God, how he had missed Alli! They'd been together for over six years. And he had no complaints about their relationship. He loved having her at his side. Whether it was in his bed or at a function, they were attending. He'd been an idiot to let her walk out of his life. Every day since she left, he'd wanted to call her, but it hurt his male ego that she'd not only walked out on him and on what they had, but also hadn't come back. Yes, his male pride was hurt. He'd never expected it to go on this long, in fact every day he'd mentally prayed she'd call.

What was apparent now was that he'd been a fool. Women thought differently than men did when it came to children. And he knew her biological time clock was ticking. Hell, they were both thirty, now. Men didn't have to worry about that time clock but women did. She wanted to have kids. She'd brought up the conversation plenty of times and he'd kept saying later. He realized she wouldn't even marry him now, unless they could have children. And the sooner the better as far as she was concerned.

She had worn the necklace he'd given her for Christmas last year. He'd gotten that hint, too. It was in the jewelry box she'd opened expecting an engagement ring. But no, he hadn't given her what she'd wanted or expected. The necklace was an exquisite piece of jewelry. It was a one of a kind, custom piece he'd specially ordered. When she'd opened the box and he'd seen the look on her face, he'd felt like a total ass. They couldn't come to an agreement about children, so he hadn't felt he could propose. So he hadn't. That was basically why they were in the predicament they were in now.

During the last six months, he'd spent a lot of time thinking about having a family with Alli. There wasn't anyone else he'd want to have his child, but did it have to be now? Maybe no one was ever ready to be a father. *Maybe you just have to do it and figure it out as you go.* That's what Alli had tried to tell him on various occasions. Now, whenever he saw small children he wondered what their child would look like. He had every confidence they would make awesome babies.

When she walked into the bowling alley last night, he immediately saw the necklace. Hell, he couldn't help notice it sitting proudly on her smooth tan skin just above her breasts that were strutting boldly up and slightly over her low cut top. It made a statement without her saying a word about the silent discussion they were not going to have at that time.

An hour later, he was in his kitchen, prepping the food for their dinner. Everything was ready to go and he'd even picked up some flowers for the table, which he would send home with her when she left. Hopefully, that would be tomorrow morning or maybe not until Monday morning. If he got really lucky, they could spend the weekend together. He'd really missed her. In fact, he really hated living in what he'd come to call *their townhouse* alone.

The doorbell rang.

"Come on in," Sam called out.

Alli opened the door and walked in. She smiled and set her purse down on the floor next to the couch before coming into the kitchen. "It smells good," she said and sat down on a stool at the bar counter.

"Hope you're hungry," Sam said.

"You know I would never pass up one of your steak dinners."

The steaks were a perfect medium. He served up the meal on plates and set them on the dining room table. Alli followed him in and took a seat opposite Sam. He poured two glasses of wine and handed one to Alli. "I forgot how nice it is to have a quiet dinner with you. You know I always enjoyed your company."

"I missed talking to you," Alli said.

After dinner, Alli helped clear the table and clean up, before they settled down on the couch. Just like an old married couple. Sam put his arm around Alli and pulled her over to snuggle while they watched the latest James Bond movie. They were both huge fans of James Bond although they disagreed on which Bond was the best Bond. Her favorite was the latest, Daniel Craig, and his was, Sean Connery. Before they got to the end, he kissed Alli and one thing led to another and before they knew it, he was carrying her to the bedroom. They swiftly shed their clothes and fell back on the bed with arms wrapped around each other.

In the morning, they mutually decided to spend the day together. There was an art festival down on the river in Stillwater. They got out of bed and showered together.

"I don't suppose you brought any extra clothes with you?" Sam asked.

"Funny you should ask. Yes. But the bag is down in my car. Would you mind running outside and getting it?" Alli asked.

"Well, we sure don't want you going outside to get it like that, now do we?" Sam said laughing and tugging at her towel.

"Sam?" she called out.

"I'll be right back. Don't you go anywhere." He was already on his way outside.

Minutes later, Sam handed Alli her bag and after she was dressed, they left in Sam's car. He pulled into the parking lot of Starbucks, right down the street.

"Thank you. You remember how badly I need my morning Starbucks."

"How could I, when you got me hooked on the darn stuff?" Sam asked as they got out of the car.

Finally an hour later, they arrived at the art show. The tents were lined up along the river, the sun was shining brightly, the temperature outside was around seventy degrees…a perfect day. They walked hand in hand past the tents before stopping to sit on a park bench overlooking the river.

"Sam, what do you think the odds are that we will end up married when the six months is up?" Alli asked.

This was his perfect opportunity to come clean and tell her. He was silent a few minutes. "We love each other, so I'd guess the chances are pretty good."

Alli smiled and kissed him. "That's exactly what I needed to hear."

Damn, but he was such a chicken shit! He should simply tell her, but then she'd want to know why he didn't tell her right away. It was only last week, but he'd made the decision to not say anything and now he was stuck. No sense causing a scene now. No, it was definitely better to basically wait it out at this point and see what happened.

Alli spent the night at Sam's again. It was exactly like old times. But were they really back together again? Maybe he could buy her the ring and they could plan a wedding. Having a baby could possibly be put off for a few years still. Right now, he was merely enjoying every minute of being with Alli. He just wasn't completely sold on the baby thing, yet. He knew he wanted Alli, but he honestly couldn't say he was excited to be a father. Yet. But keeping Alli in his life was something he was prepared to do almost anything to make happen. Maybe it really could end up being a moot point? He had friends who had waited to have children and then found out they couldn't have children or they would have to spend thousands of dollars to make it happen. And sometimes, it still didn't happen.

Sunday morning, Alli left to go to church. Sam didn't go with her. He loved her church, but they weren't 100% back together yet and he didn't want to start the tongues wagging about their relationship. Alli took her bag, as she wasn't going to be spending the night again.

After Alli left, he sat on the couch feeling totally lost. She'd only just left and he felt like it had been years. She could move back in with him, but then again she'd said that would not happen until they saw how the next six months went. Meaning, they needed to be engaged.

This all meant he needed to be sure about them if he asked her to move back in with him. He needed to buy an engagement ring and set a wedding date or it totally wasn't going to happen. Hell, he totally wanted it to be the way it was before. Alli was his soul mate, he knew that. Now especially, after the separation. The sex between them was always great because they had such a strong physical attraction to each other which made it hard to keep their hands off one another. But even more than that he missed talking to her. He wanted to spend the rest of his life talking to her each and every day.

And now that they were actually married, it really complicated things. All he knew was that he wanted her with him. The only other problem was she didn't know they were married and he needed to figure out a way to tell her. Or did he? If he proposed and they set a date, they could have the big church wedding she'd always dreamed about and maybe he wouldn't ever have to tell her. Actually, the more he thought about it that made the most sense. Why tell her if he didn't need to? He really didn't have a clue what her reaction would be, but why take a chance that she would be upset? Women were just so unpredictable. So why take the chance? No, there was no reason to tell her at all once they were engaged.

CHAPTER 11

*A*fter church, Alli checked the messages on her phone and saw multiple messages from Susie. She pressed return call.

"Susie—"

"Alli, where have you been? You didn't return my calls. I was worried."

"I told you I was having dinner with Sam."

"Yes, that was Friday and today is Sunday. Don't tell me you spent the weekend at his place. Your old place. Oh, you know what I mean."

"Yes, and it was perfect. Basically like we never broke up."

"Great. Did you two talk about getting married?"

"I gave him six months and it's only been a week. I think he's coming around. I think he will propose before the six months is up."

"Well, I hope so for your sake. So if he does, how far out are you going to set the date?"

"It'll be soon. I'm not going to give him time to change his mind. We're doing it right away. I've waited long enough."

"Does he even know you had already bought the wedding dress?" Susie asked.

"No. You know I never told him. It's paid for, but it's still at the bridal shop. She asked me if I wanted her to try and sell it, but I simply couldn't do it. That dress is perfect for me, it's my dream wedding dress." Alli walked to her car.

"So once he proposes, everything is still in place from before? The Wilds Golf Club for the reception, the bridesmaid dresses, etc."

"Yup. I've waited six and a half years for this wedding, so once he proposes, I think I will set the date two months out."

"But what if The Wilds Golf Club isn't available?"

"I sincerely hope it will be, but if it isn't I'll have to deal with it and find another place. But I really want to have it there, so we'll see what happens."

"Okay, I sure hope you know what you're getting yourself into."

"I'm off to do some errands now, so have to go. Talk to you later," Alli said and ended the call.

The weeks passed quickly and before she knew it, two months had passed. Her relationship with Sam had progressed steadily to the point she spent every weekend at his place and stayed at her place during the week.

There was only one thing bothering her. She'd been off the pill for the past three months and her periods were irregular to say the least. She'd stayed on the pill, initially thinking they would get back together. Sooner rather than later. When it appeared that wouldn't happen, she made an appointment to see her doctor who suggested it was a good time to go off the pill. At least for the time being. So she had. When she spent the first weekend with Sam, he'd asked if she was still on the pill and she told him she wasn't. So they'd used condoms which weren't hers or Sam's favorite form of birth control.

She'd made an appointment for a checkup with her doctor to get a new prescription for the Pill. So here she sat in the doctor's office, waiting for the nurse to come in.

"Alli, please use the restroom down the hall to give us a urine spec-imen. There are containers available in the wall cabinet."

"Thanks," Alli said.

The nurse left and Alli walked down to the restroom. This may well be the longest walk of her life. When the doctor had asked if there was any chance she could be pregnant, she was thrown for a minute. Her first instinct was to say, no. But then the doctor asked if she'd had any unprotected sex which gave her cause for concern. Once, she'd said. Nobody got pregnant having sex one time. Did they? She'd heard people tell stories about women who had but to be perfectly honest she never believed it. Nobody was that naïve. But that night in Vegas was totally unplanned and it was over two months ago. She was pretty damn sure they hadn't used a condom. She was drunk and so was he.

Damn! There obviously was a very slim chance she could be pregnant. Hell, she had no idea where she was in her cycle since it had been so irregular after going off the pill. What were the odds she'd been ovulating that very night? Well, she was about to find out.

Alli filled the container and put it in the cabinet door on the wall of the restroom where the lab techs could test it. Hell, she could've stopped at Walgreens and bought a pregnancy tester herself, but as long as she was here, she might as well have them do it.

Back in the exam room, she sat waiting for the doctor to come in with the results. What would Sam say if she was pregnant? Damn it, it was just as much his fault as hers. Really wasn't anyone's fault. No, it would be up to fate.

It seemed like hours, but about ten minutes later the doctor walked in. "Alli, you won't be needing that prescription for the Pill. You're pregnant."

"Oh, my God."

"I hope this is good news. You did say you and Sam are back together again and I know how badly you wanted to have a baby."

"Yes, we are. I'm not sure he will be happy."

"Regardless what he decides, you *will* be having the baby, right?"

"No question about it."

"Great. We need to get you on some prenatal vitamins and if you have any problems with nausea, let us know. Set up an appointment in a month."

"When's the due date?" Alli asked.

"Well, you made this easy since you know exactly when the baby was conceived."

"Yes, nine months from Sam's birthday. So that puts the due date around March 30."

Alli walked out of the doctor's office in a daze. When she reached her car, she got in and the tears rolled down her cheeks. Why was she crying? This should be one of the happiest days of her life. And yes, she was happy about the baby. She would love this baby for her whole lifetime, but the question was whether she would still be able to spend the rest of her life with Sam? What would Sam do when he found out she was pregnant? Run for the hills? Think it was the best thing that ever happened to him?

There absolutely was no way she could tell him. What she needed to do was get him to propose to her and quickly. Very quickly! She really had no desire to walk down the aisle pregnant. So the sooner the better, as her stomach would only continue to grow.

Now whether to tell anyone else? Her parents lived in Dallas meaning her mother wouldn't be around to notice she was putting on weight, so she could wait a bit. Susie was another thing entirely. She was her best friend and knew everything about her. In fact, they'd grown up together and even went to college together at Mankato State. And Susie would definitely notice if she put on any weight. Gaining weight was inevitable in this situation. But she wasn't sure Susie would be able to keep it from Sam. She had to tell someone though. She felt too excited despite the circumstances. She'd dreamt about having Sam's baby for way too long. This was a dream come true and she deserved to be happy.

Alli tapped her phone to call Susie. "Hi."

"Alli, what's going on?" Susie asked.

"Can you stop over after work tonight?" Alli asked.

"Sure. Are you okay?"

"Yah, I'm great actually. I just need to talk to you." Alli hesitated, but didn't say anything more.

"Okay, I'll see you around six."

Alli stopped to pick up her pre-natal vitamins on the way home. She'd left work early for her doctor's appointment and it wouldn't pay to go back into the office, so she stopped at the Mall Of America to do some window shopping since she had a couple of hours to kill. She came across a baby store and walked inside. The clerk smiled and welcomed her to the store. Alli was ecstatic that she, finally, would be able to buy some of these wonderful little people clothes. But not today. It was too soon.

At six, Susie knocked on her door and let herself in. She walked over and gave Alli a hug. "Everything okay, kiddo?"

"I'm great. Let's sit down." Alli walked over and sat on the couch.

Susie joined her. "Alli, I'm dying here. What's going on?"

"Well, remember how my period got all screwed up when I went off the Pill?"

"Yes."

"And that night in Vegas on Sam's birthday when we had crazy hot sex?" Alli asked.

"Oh my God! Alli, tell me you used a condom."

"No condom."

"Alli! What were you thinking?"

"Hell, we were drunk and the chemistry was over the top."

"Alli?" Susie asked.

"I'm pregnant!" Alli announced.

Susie's mouth dropped open as she seemed at a loss for words at the moment. Finally, she asked, "Are we happy about this?"

"Ecstatic."

Susie reached over to hug and practically squeeze Alli to death. "I know how long you've wanted this, but I know you wanted to be married first. So what about Sam? Does he know?"

"No, he doesn't know. I'm not sure I'm going to tell him until he at least proposes first."

"Well, that needs to be sooner rather than later. When are you due?"

"End of March."

"So how do you propose to get him to pop the question?" Susie asked.

"Not a clue. If he doesn't and we don't get married, I'm still having the baby. It's not like I tricked him or anything. If I have to, I'll raise our baby alone."

"Let's hope you don't have to," Susie said as Alli handed her a baby magazine to look at and picked up another for herself. They'd both been waiting a long time to have a reason to look at baby magazines.

CHAPTER 12

*I*t had been getting harder and harder for Alli to keep from saying anything to Sam about the baby. They were going on the third month of her six month ultimatum. She'd breached the marriage subject a couple of times but hadn't made any headway. The nausea would come and go, but luckily she'd never actually thrown up yet.

As far as having a wedding, she kept working on her dream wedding plans. She wanted to have everything planned, so when or if Sam proposed, everything would be ready to go. Tonight after work, she was meeting Susie at the Wedding Cake Perfecto shop to taste cakes.

Susie pulled into the parking lot only minutes behind Alli. "Are sure you want to do this?"

"Absolutely," Alli said.

"But—"

"I know," Alli cut her off. "What if he doesn't propose?"

"Exactly! Then what?" Susie asked.

"Funny, you should ask that question. Because I have come up with another option."

"And what might that be?" Susie asked as she stood absolutely still waiting for Alli's response.

"I'm going to propose to him," Alli stated proudly.

"You're not serious, are you?" Susie asked with pleading eyes.

"Dead serious." Alli started walking toward the shop.

Susie followed behind her. "I can see you have thought this through. So there is probably no talking you out of it, right?"

"Nothing you can say will change my mind."

"So when are you going to do this?" Susie asked.

"This weekend."

"That is awfully soon."

"I know. But pretty soon my pregnancy will become obvious to him. My God, we sleep together. He'll notice if I gain any weight. My breasts are already extremely tender. And I'm sure he's wondering why I have declined to have a glass of wine each time he's asked me."

"You're right. I know that's been hard, but I'm so scared for you, Alli. He might say *No* and then what?" Susie asked.

"Well, I've thought of that, too. If he does, we'll basically have a smaller version of the wedding without him. Then he'll feel like a real ass, for missing his own wedding."

"Right. So do you have a proposal all planned out? Or are you simply going to come right out and ask him?" Susie asked.

"I told him I would make dinner on Saturday night. That way we'll be at my place, so if it all goes to Hell, he can just leave. Then I don't have to drive anywhere while I'm crying my eyes out."

"I think you're right, it's probably best to get it over with. Then you'll know where you stand and you can get on with your life."

"I'm going to ask him after we have the hottest sex ever. I bought a sexy new bra and matching thong, downloaded some of our favorite love songs, and I'm making a to-die-for decadent chocolate cake for dessert."

"Sounds like a good plan."

"If he says no, then we're done and he will walk out of my life that night for good. There will be no looking back."

"Okay, let's go taste some cake. I've always thought chocolate would be the way to go. None of that prissy white stuff for me, but hey it's your choice," Susie said.

They walked into the shop and before they knew it, they were practically drowning in wedding cakes. Although, it was the Chocolate Almond that seemed to be both of their undoing. It was simply ecstasy without sex.

～

DUSTIN AND SAM were at *Champps Kitchen & Bar* in Eden Prairie watching the Vikings football game.

"Hell, it would really be nice to watch them win one of these games," Sam said.

"Why do we keep watching them? Maybe we should pick a different team to watch?"

"Like the Green Bay Packers?"

"That would be so bad, and we'd be traitors."

"Hey, at least we could say our team won a few games," Sam said.

"So what's going on with you and Alli?" Dustin asked.

"We're pretty much back together. She spends the weekends at my place."

"So is she moving back in soon?"

"I hope so," Sam said, half watching the game.

"Don't you have to propose first or something?" Dustin asked.

"Yup. Damn, but don't we have anyone on that team who can throw the ball without giving it to the other team?"

"Sam! You really gonna do it this time?" Dustin asked not taking his eyes off of the big screen TV.

"Think so, man," Sam said while still watching the game.

"You sure about this?" Dustin asked.

"Actually never been more sure about anything."

"You must really love her," Dustin surmised.

"Didn't know how much until she left," Sam stated matter-of-factly.

"Buy a ring?" Dustin asked.

"She had one she'd shown me before we broke up. She wanted it for Christmas last year, but I gave her a necklace instead. I'm picking it up Wednesday after work."

"Wow! You are really going to do this," Dustin said.

"I am."

"So do you have some memorable way you're going to do it?" Dustin asked.

"I was going to take her out to dinner at Ocean Air on Saturday night, but she said she wanted to cook dinner on Saturday night at her place. So I'm going to take her there on Friday night instead."

"You know she's going to want to get married right away."

"Might as well get it over with. Hell, we lived together for over six years, so I know exactly what I'll be getting."

"That's true."

"Touchdown!" Sam yelled along with everyone in the bar.

"Alli is a great catch, and you two make the perfect couple," Dustin said.

"You know by this time next year, I'll be a married man," Sam said and a smile stretched across his face. God, he loved Alli and he couldn't wait to spend the rest of his life with her. She was beautiful both inside and out and she was his. There was no way he would let her go this time. No one had to tell him to not make the same mistake twice. He was definitely doing it right this time.

Sam texted Alli's phone.

I'm taking you to dinner on Friday night at the Ocean Air restaurant downtown Minneapolis. Wear one of your sexy little black dresses, we're going to make it a night to remember!

CHAPTER 13

*A*lli had just walked in the door to her apartment when she heard her phone do its dinging sound, meaning she'd received a text. She closed the door and dug the phone out of her purse that she'd just set on the counter. Her finger tapped the screen and the text popped up. It was from Sam. She read it and smiled. He wanted to take her out to dinner at a fancy smancy restaurant on Friday night. And he wanted her to wear a sexy little black dress. *Wonder what's on his mind?* She smiled because she had a pretty good idea. Hot, steamy, mind blowing sex after dinner. Exactly what she had in mind for Saturday night.

Well, he was stealing her idea, but she was fairly certain he wasn't going to propose. Oh well, they could have hot steamy sex on Saturday night, too. And then she was going to propose. *It isn't that crazy of an idea, is it? What about all this empowerment to women? Equality for men and women?* She knew what she wanted and she wanted Sam. And the baby, of course. It would definitely be a weekend to remember and hopefully to tell her future children about.

She'd just set the phone down when it rang. She walked back to the counter and looked to see who was calling. Her mother. She hesitated for a moment and then tapped the phone to answer the call. "Mom."

"How are you doing, Alli? Haven't heard from you for a while, everything okay up in Minnesota?"

"I'm just busy, Mom. Sorry, I haven't called."

"Your dad and I are thinking about coming back to Minneapolis for Christmas this year. Thought it would be nice to spend Christmas in Minnesota for a change and hopefully see some snow."

"I'd love to have you up here with me and Sam for Christmas."

"You and Sam?" her mom asked incredulously.

"Yes, we're back together," Alli said.

"Why didn't you call and tell us?"

"I wanted to make sure it worked out first."

"When did you get back together?"

"It's been three months now."

"Is it working out?"

"I think it's going to work for us this time."

"I assume this is what you want?"

"Mom, you know I love Sam and have wanted to marry him for quite a while."

"I know, baby, but does he feel the same?"

"Sam loves me, he basically got scared to take the next step to marriage."

"Well, we have to run, we're off to see a show. I'll let you know our flight schedule after we book the tickets. Can't wait to see you and Sam."

"Bye," Alli said and ended the call.

Great. . . she hadn't expected that. Her parents hadn't been back up to Minneapolis during Christmas for a long time, in fact, it had been before she'd met Sam. Odd, they'd chosen this year to come. Not that she didn't want her parents to come and visit, she did. She only hoped she could tell them about the engagement before telling her mom she would be a grandmother. Her mother was not the baby type and had a hard time acting her age. She was after all in her mid-fifties and acted like she thought she was still in her forties. She would wait till she got their flight schedule from them to tell Sam. After she knew for sure they were really coming. No sense stirring the pot for nothing.

Alli took the afternoon off on Friday, so she could do a little shopping. And maybe find a new little black dress to wear. Last night she had tried on a few of her dresses and they were a little tight across the bust. So if she could find a new one, she would feel better. She didn't want her dress to focus on her slightly increasing waist, bust, and weight.

She stopped at the mall and lucked out at the second store she walked into. It was black, short and fit perfect. Alli knew it wouldn't fit for long, but it fit now and it made her look super sexy which is exactly what she was looking for. She wanted Sam to be damn sure he knew how lucky he was to have her. And not only her body, but also her love and commitment for life.

Alli then became a nervous wreck the rest of the day on Friday. Finally, it was time to get dressed for her big night with Sam. She took extra time with her make-up and hair. Everything needed to be perfect. She didn't want Sam to doubt for one minute, that she was the woman for him. She sprayed her neck and wrists with cologne and then slid the dress on. Her four inch heels were black leather and strappy. Good thing Sam was tall. She stood in front of the full length mirror checking her reflection to make sure everything looked perfect. She liked what she saw and prayed Sam would, too.

CHAPTER 14

S am left work early to stop by the jewelry store. He pulled up and parked in front.

"Sam," the jeweler greeted him when he walked in the door.

"Dan, is it ready?" Sam asked.

"It's ready to dazzle, Alli," he said and held the ring out for Sam to inspect.

Sam took the ring and watched as it sparkled in his hand. Alli was going to be ecstatic when she saw it. "Looks like it should do the job," Sam said and handed it back to Dan.

He put it in a ring box then put it in a bag.

Sam laid his credit card on the counter and waited as it slid through the side of the machine.

Dan laid the slip on the counter for him to sign and handed the card back to Sam.

"Thanks. This will make Alli very happy," Sam said and walked out of the store.

Driving home, he thought about how different the last six months could've been for him and Alli if he'd simply bought the ring for her last Christmas, instead of the necklace. They'd lost six months. Not much he could do about it now. He was correcting the situation tonight, so their lives could go on and move forward instead of backwards.

Dustin was the only one who knew he was doing this. Proposing to Alli tonight, that is. After it was official, he would let the rest of the guys know then call his mother and dad. His mom was pretty hip and into all the new technology, so maybe he'd send her a picture of Alli and the ring on his phone tonight.

Dustin thought he was doing the right thing. Sam *knew* he was doing the right thing and he really didn't care what anyone else thought. It was his life. And Alli's. Plus, it was time to do the right thing and marry her.

After he got back to his place, he showered, put on Alli's favorite Men's cologne followed by his dress shirt and suit. He wanted to look good.

Sam arrived a half an hour early, just in case Alli was early. He didn't want her to have to wait for him. So he waited in the lobby. He observed as both men and women came through the door. Many young business types trying to relax and socialize after work, he surmised. Some couples walked in holding hands. They must be in love, he thought. A smile spread across his face as his mind focused on Alli and how much he loved her.

The restaurant catered to the more affluent yuppie class. One of the most expensive restaurants in town, but he could afford it. Besides, he wanted this night to be extra special for Alli. The décor on the mahogany wood walls was adorned with exquisite ocean ships and beaches art hung effectively throughout the seating area.

At five to seven, Alli walked into the Ocean Air restaurant.

He was mesmerized as he watched her long sleek and very tan legs appear in the doorway firmly encased in black leather stilettos. The little black dress fit her like a glove, showing off every curve of her beautiful body. Her long blonde hair floated gently around her bare shoulders as the delicate curls moved along with the motion of her body while she walked toward him.

Damn, he was already hard and totally ready to take her to the paradise only they could find together.

She enticingly approached him and stopped only inches from him. Her breasts glistened as they rose above the low cut front of the dress.

He couldn't help it, his eyes lowered to the feast he most certainly would be enjoying later. He looked up into her stunning brown eyes.

A sexy and enticing smile spread across her face as their eyes met. Damn, she knew he would be ogling her breasts. She deliberately wanted him to.

He could see it in her eyes. Sam pulled her gently even closer towards him and gave her a quick kiss. He took her hand and they walked over to check in for their reservation. The hostess nodded in the direction of the window tables and they followed her. The view from their table was absolutely spectacular. The lights of downtown and the stone Arch Bridge appeared as beacons of light casting a truly romantic spell.

Sam leaned in and whispered in Alli's ear, "You look beautiful."

"Thanks," she responded. "You look pretty good yourself."

They sat down at the table and she continued to glance toward the river decked out in its light spectacle of glory.

Sam ordered a bottle of wine and the waiter left. "So how was your day?"

"Just a usual day at work, nothing out of the ordinary."

"Mine, too. Glad it's Friday and we get to spend the weekend together." He reached out to hold her hand. "Alli, you look absolutely breathtaking tonight. It's almost like you have this glow about you."

Alli shifted in her chair. "Sam, you're probably making me blush."

The waiter brought the wine and poured them each a glass. They both took a sip to taste it and set the glasses back down on the table. The menu was filled with many delicious choices, but the Lobster and steak combos which were there favorites, ultimately won out.

After dinner, they ordered Mud Pie for dessert. It was enough for two so they shared the mocha frozen ice cream pie topped with a warm decadent chocolate sauce and sprinkled with almonds.

Sam was eager to leave after dinner as he had an important agenda to take care of. He walked Alli to her car with his arm firmly around her waist. At her car, he pulled her into his arms for a passionate deep kiss that promised what was ahead for them on this special evening. "I'll follow you to my place," he said as he ended the kiss and walked to his car.

They parked and walked into his place with arms around each other. Alli walked in the open door with Sam right behind her. As soon as they were clear of the door, Sam pushed the door shut behind him. He pulled Alli to him and kissed her lips, then neck and shoulder. She looked so hot and sexy, he couldn't wait to get her into bed so he could literally ravish her body and give her earth-shattering orgasms. He picked her up and carried her to the bedroom. This totally wasn't going as planned. He was so turned on he was debating on proposing after he ravished her body, but he knew he needed to do it first.

Sam took her hand and led her back out to the living room, gently setting her down on the leather couch then sat down beside her.

To say Alli looked a bit confused was definitely an understatement. "Everything all right, Sam?"

"Couldn't be better. In fact, I have something to say to you first before I get sidetracked and we end up back in the bedroom." He picked up her hand and held it in his. "Alli, I have loved you since the day we met, well over six years ago. You are my best friend and a fabulous lover. I must have been insane to let you walk away last January. I regretted it immediately. Unfortunately, I thought you would come back or call after a couple days, but days led to months and we were both too stubborn to give in. I wish I would've called you back the next day, but we can't change the past, only the future."

"Sam—"

Sam held up his other hand to stop her. "Let me finish. Alli, I love you and want to spend the rest of my life with you." He reached into his pocket, pulled out the ring box, then opened it. Holding it in one hand, he watched her face. "Alli, will you marry me?"

Tears were already falling from Alli's eyes as she said, "Yes, I love you with all my heart and I want to spend the rest of my life with you."

Sam took the ring out of the box and slid it on her finger. Alli wrapped her arms around him then kissed him as if she would never let him go. Sam picked her up again, carried her to the bedroom, and laid her on the bed. He laid down next to her, continuing to ravish her body with kisses on her lips, neck then he found her breasts as the zipper went down on the dress...they were finally free from their confines and eager to be suckled.

Minutes later, they broke the embrace as Alli got up to remove her dress and shoes. Sam shed his pants, shirt and shoes. Undies were on the floor next and they were naked on the bed with flushed bodies utterly dying to be joined together as one. Sam stopped to put a condom on and proceeded to eagerly plunge into Alli's waiting haven of sheer ecstasy. Shortly after, they both climaxed together.

"Alli, I love you," Sam said as he rolled to his side.

Alli rolled over onto his chest. "I love you, Sam." She kissed him and they fell asleep in each other's arms.

ALLI WOKE the next morning wrapped in Sam's arms. God, how she loved this man. And he had proposed! She was ecstatic. He loved her and wanted to spend the rest of their lives together. *What more could a girl ask for?*

Something kept nagging at her though. He'd said he knew their break up was a mistake. But the one thing he hadn't mentioned was having children. And that was the reason they'd broken up. Maybe, he simply hadn't thought about it last night, since it probably wasn't foremost on his mind. It, however, was constantly in her thoughts and overwhelmingly in her body. Well, she refused to ruin the best day of her life, by worrying about it. He must've changed his mind meaning he would be okay with it or he wouldn't have proposed. *Right?* But what if he hadn't? Maybe, she should wait to tell him? Maybe, it would be best to be married first? Then, if he hadn't changed his mind beforehand, he would, since they would already be married. And hopefully very happy. Yes, that's what she needed to do. Plan the wedding and get married as soon as possible. She could tell him on the honeymoon. Sam loved her she knew that. Once they were married, he would be okay with the baby and becoming a father. *Right?*

CHAPTER 15

*A*lli thought about going back to sleep, but more sleep was not to be. Sam, her new fiancé, was eager to start the morning off by making love to her. Obviously, she would not decline an obviously sex starved man. Momentarily, Alli wondered if Sam had slept with anyone else while they were broken up, but right now this wasn't something she wanted to know.

She rolled over on her side to face him so she could kiss him good morning.

Almost immediately, Sam was hovering over her still kissing her. He smiled and continued working himself downward until a firm breast was within reach of his mouth. He kissed and suckled it until Alli was writhing beneath him, as their bodies moved in unison. Then he entered her and they both reached exquisite orgasms.

As they lay exhausted and satisfied, Alli couldn't help thinking about how they'd ended up here. In his bed. Engaged. She turned her hand over so she could look at the rock on her finger. The same ring she'd picked out almost a year ago. She felt totally amazed to think he'd actually been paying attention at that time and even more that he'd remembered the ring. Set in gold, the center stone was about two carats she would guess. It was so beautiful! She loved it! And most of all she loved Sam.

She turned over and laid on her back as Sam turned on his side and slid his hand caressingly over her flat stomach.

Alli enjoyed his caresses but she knew soon, her now flat stomach would not be so flat. She would have to tell him probably sooner rather than later. But not today. "Sam, now that we are officially engaged, we need to set a date."

"How long will it take to plan a wedding?" Sam asked.

"You probably weren't aware that in anticipation of becoming engaged last Christmas, I had begun making wedding preparations."

"Alli, I am so sorry I screwed up last Christmas," Sam said and kissed her. "Can you forgive me?"

"If you'd asked me that before your birthday, the answer would've been—no." But, as of the events of last night, you are forgiven," Alli said and gave him light feather kisses on his lips.

Sam pulled Alli into his arms for a passionate kiss. "I'm never letting you go again."

I hope not, Alli thought. But his promise gave her hope that he had come around to his thinking on starting a family. Only time would tell. And she intended to use as much time as she could to solidify their relationship before she told him. "I've been waiting a long time, the sooner the better. If that's okay with you?" Alli asked.

"I remember you talked about having the reception at The Wilds Country Club, did you still want to have it there?"

"Yes."

"Well, why don't you check and see if they have any dates open in the next few months and we'll go from there?" Sam smiled at her.

"Great! I will call them on Monday. So if they have something open, should I reserve it?" Alli asked.

"Yes, by all means have them put us down. I will leave it up to you. I know you women like to plan everything out for your dream wedding, so go for it. Just let me know if you want me to help you with anything or if you want me to take care of something. Okay?"

"Don't worry, I will. Susie, of course, will be my maid of honor and will be happy to help with my planning." Alli laughed. "I think she will be more than ecstatic to help."

"So, I suppose we should get out of bed sometime before noon," Sam said as he stood up and tossed a pillow at Alli.

"Okay! I'm getting up," she said and followed Sam into the shower.

While they were dressing, Sam asked, "How about heading over to The Wilds Golf Club for brunch and we can take a look at the place?"

"Great idea!" Alli said then finished putting on her make-up and drying her hair. "I'll be ready in fifteen minutes." She put on a pair of jean capris, a tank top and a long light open wrap sweater. Thankfully, she'd brought her overnight bag along. Lastly, she put on a pair of cream colored sandals with three inch heels.

It was late September, but the weather was unseasonably warm. But hey, she wasn't complaining at all. She liked the warm weather.

They pulled into a very full parking lot at The Wilds Golf Club, but managed to get a spot from someone just leaving. The Wilds Golf Club was the golf course's club house, so it was surrounded by water fountains with lush green grass and shrubberies. Alli had her eye on this place for quite a few years. The décor shouted class. But the best part was the food. The Wilds Golf Club employed special chefs who worked the Sunday brunch and weddings, so the food was exceptional.

The hostess gave them a table by the window after they expressed they were there to check out The Wilds Golf Club for a wedding reception. Since the weather had been warm, the trees had only started turning their bright reds, golds and rusts of the autumn hues. It was beautiful. Alli couldn't believe she was sitting here with her fiancé, Sam. Only a few months ago if anyone had told her she'd be engaged to Sam, she would have laughed. But here she was. And her dream was about to come true.

The brunch came complete with ice sculptures and beautiful floral arrangements in the current fall colors. They filled their plates with delicious breakfast items first—hash browns, bacon, eggs, French toast and fresh fruit. The strawberries and watermelon were her choices. When they returned to their table, they found a basket of warm cinnamon rolls.

Both Alli and Sam were famished. They weren't kidding when they say sex was good exercise. Plus, she was eating for two. Alli set her plate down and went back to get them both fresh squeezed orange juice mimosas. She knew Sam would get them, but she wanted to go, since she could get a plain orange juice for herself and the mimosa which included champagne for Sam.

"I do like this place," Sam said.

"The outside patio will be great for people to cool off after dancing," Alli said looking out the window.

"This is a great location, Alli. Maybe we can check to see if anyone in the event coordinating office is here today. You never know, they may have an event here later today."

"Won't hurt to check," Alli agreed.

After they finished their breakfast items, they went up for the dinner items. There was a large selection of items, including turkey, ham, salmon, mashed potatoes, vegetables, dressing, wild rice soup and a table full of desserts. Various pies, cookies and bars filled the table. And to top all that off, they had an ice cream machine to make sundaes.

Alli was beginning to get full, but heck there was always room for dessert, so she filled a plate with different kinds of pies and bars. She set it in the center of the table where they both could taste each one. They managed to clean the plate, not leaving a single crumb on it.

Sam paid the bill and they walked down the hallway to look for the event coordinator's office. It was at the end of the hallway. Sam knocked on the closed door and they were both surprised when someone opened the door.

"Hi, can I help you?" the young woman asked.

"Yes, sorry to bother you on Sunday, but we just had brunch and felt this would be a perfect place to have our wedding reception. If you have a moment, we'd like to see what or if you have any dates available in November by any chance?" Alli asked.

"I'm Cindy. Come on in and have a seat. I have an event later today, which is why I'm here right now. I can certainly take a look in the book to see. I know we were pretty booked up, but I do believe we had a cancelation come in last week." Cindy walked over to her desk and opened her appointment book. "Yes, here it is. We had a cancellation for November 15."

Alli looked at Sam with a tear glistening in the corner of her eye. "What do think, Sam?"

"It sounds perfect."

"We'll take it," Alli said.

"Great. I simply need you to fill out this form with your info and then I'll need a check for $500.00 to hold it." She handed Alli the form.

Minutes later, they walked out with a folder filled with all the vital information they would need to plan a wedding reception at The Wilds Golf Club.

Once in the hall, Alli threw her arms around Sam, hugged him, and kissed him soundly on the lips. "I'm so excited! We're really getting married! And we're having the reception exactly where I wanted to have it. At The Wilds Golf Club!"

Sam held her in his arms. "Me, too," he said and kissed her.

CHAPTER 16

*M*onday morning on the way to work, Sam called Dustin.

"Sam. Kinda early for you isn't it?"

"I did it."

"Really. Guess you're out of circulation for good, Man," Dustin stated matter-of-factly.

"Alli is extremely happy about it," Sam said.

"She liked the ring, huh," Dustin said.

"She'd better. It's the one she picked out."

"So did she make you pick a date already?" Dustin asked.

"Damn straight! I don't think she's taking any chances on me changing my mind about it."

"So when's the big day?" Dustin asked.

"November 15."

"Boy, she isn't wasting any time!"

"We had brunch at The Wilds Golf Club yesterday, and I was shocked to hear the event lady say they'd just gotten a cancelation for November 15."

"So it's at The Wilds Golf Club then," Dustin stated.

"I need to call the pastor today to make sure the church is available," Sam said.

"And if it isn't?"

"Not so sure Alli has a plan B for the church," Sam said.

"Do you think she'd have it at a different one?" Dustin asked.

"Hell, I don't know. Guess we'll have to cross that bridge when we come to it. Then I need to apply for the wedding license."

"Sounds like you have a *To Do* list already. Well, congratulations Sam."

"Gotta go. Later," Sam said.

After lunch, Sam called the church to talk to the pastor, but he wasn't there so he asked the receptionist if she could check the calendar to see if a certain date was available. To his utter disbelief, November 15th was. He made an appointment on Thursday evening for both him and Alli to come in for a pre-marriage session. He didn't really think he needed one. He knew everything he needed to know about Alli and how to make their relationship work. Of course, in his opinion, it would work out best if they waited at least five years before having children. He knew Alli would never go for that, but what the heck, he could always give it a shot.

THURSDAY EVENING he met Alli at their church, St. Paul's Lutheran. They both knew the pastor since they'd joined the church about five years ago.

"Come on in," the Pastor said.

Alli and Sam walked into the pastor's office. An hour later, they had the wedding ceremony planned out, including every tiny detail. The only thing left to do was write their own nuptials. Alli seemed very excited about that last part. But, he on the other hand wasn't so sure he even had a clue as where to begin or what to write. Alli probably had hers already written out. He wasn't stupid. He could figure it out. Maybe he could Google samples of wedding vows on the internet? Yes, that was a great idea! At least, he could get some ideas that way and rewrite it the way he wanted it to be. He felt pleased he'd thought of it.

Alli forgot to bring a change of clothes for work, so she went back to her place to sleep. Which was okay with Sam since he was exhausted. He'd had enough wedding planning for one day. Alli had been great about all the wedding plans. In fact, she'd been doing most of it herself.

It was a lot to do in a short amount of time. And he wasn't sure why they needed to get married so quickly. They could've certainly waited a little bit longer. Hell, they'd waited this long, what would a few more months hurt? Women, who could understand why they did anything? However, if this was what she wanted, then that's what he would do.

Alli apparently felt he needed another job to do on the wedding list, so in her email Friday morning, she asked him to plan the honeymoon. In his opinion, Las Vegas, would be extremely appropriate under the circumstances. And she'd said it was his choice, so Vegas it was.

CHAPTER 17

Saturday morning, Alli met Susie at the mall to look for new bridesmaid dresses since the ones she'd picked out last year were no longer available. They stopped at a few shops and were lucky to find one carrying exactly the dress style Alli had envisioned in her mind. A rust, strapless, long satin dress with a time frame of only two weeks for the store to have them ordered in. Then, of course, they would need to be altered which could take up to two weeks. It would work if there weren't any delays.

"What do you think?" Alli asked Susie.

"They're not bad at all for bridesmaid dresses and since we're on such a tight timeline, I think we should order these."

"Let's text Jennifer and Kally a photo of the dress and get their sizes." Alli pulled out her phone.

After all the paperwork was submitted and signed, they walked down to the Starbucks to check out the new Pumpkin Spice Lattes.

"What's next on the list?" Susie asked after they sat down at a table with their drinks.

"So far, we have the venue and church booked, my dress was already taken care of and the bridesmaid dresses are ordered, and the cake is taken care of. Sam said the chocolate almond sounded good to him, so I went ahead and ordered it. Only flowers left, I think."

"Do you want to do that today?"

"Yes, let's stop at Prior Lake Floral since they're close to The Wilds Golf Club."

"Is Sam taking care of the tuxes?"

"Yes, and the limo."

"Did you pick out the food already at The Wilds Golf Club?"

"Sam and I did that the day we booked the venue with them."

"Sounds like you have everything covered then. I simply have to plan a bridal shower. Are your Saturdays open in October?"

"Yes, just let me know which one so I can mark it down in my calendar."

"My condo has a really nice party room we can use. Since it's such short notice and your mom is in Dallas, we can do one big shower and invite your friends and family."

"I think that would be best. I'll get a list from my mom and Sam's mom. I need to call my mom first though and tell her about the engagement."

"You haven't told her?"

"You know how she is. I wanted to make sure everything was for sure before I told her."

"Call her tonight," Susie said.

"I will. It's on my list."

"By the way, Trevor is coming for a visit this weekend."

"Sorry, I've been so busy with this wedding stuff, I forgot to ask about your long-distance relationship. How's it going?"

"We talk every night for a couple of hours on the phone, so it will be really nice to do that in person for a change."

"I'm happy for you. Hope it works out."

"I might put together a little party so he can meet some of my friends. Would you want to stop by?"

"I'd bring Sam. Did you tell Trevor I got engaged to Sam?"

"No. The subject hasn't come up about you, but I'll be sure to tell him."

"You're my best friend. Of course, I'll come. Let me know which day, the time, and I will talk to Sam."

~

WHEN ALLI GOT HOME, she got comfy on the couch to make her phone call to her mother. She'd been putting it off because she didn't want to lie to her mom, but she couldn't tell her about the baby until she told Sam. So she would only tell her about the engagement and the wedding. She pressed her mom's number on her cell.

"Mom, I've got some good news to tell you. Sam proposed and we're getting married on November 15." Alli hadn't intended to basically blurt it all out in one sentence, but it was best to get it all out there at once.

"What? When did this happen?" her mom asked.

"Friday night."

"You didn't say yesterday, so last Friday? And you're just calling me now?"

"We decided to get married right away, so I've been busy getting everything all set up and I wanted to have a date to give you."

"Well, what do you need me to do?"

"I've been planning this wedding in my head for over six years, so I'm pretty set. I hope you can come for the shower though on October 15."

"Certainly. I'll give my sister, Gail, a call to see if I can stay with her for a few weeks. That way, I'll be able to help you with last minute details and of course, I'll plan the Rehearsal dinner."

"Great. Thanks, Mom."

"So I'm assuming Sam came around to the whole idea of being married and starting a family which is what you wanted?"

"Yes, everything is fine. He just got a little scared of what the commitment of having a family means, but he's okay with it now."

"I'm happy for you, Alli. I know how much you love Sam and this is what you've wanted. Tell me about the proposal and I want to see the ring."

Alli told her mom all about Sam's proposal and sent a text with a picture of the ring. They talked about all the plans so far with the church and The Wilds Golf Club. At the end of the call, she could tell her mom was excited and looking forward to the wedding, too. Since she'd been with Sam for over six years they knew each other's families well and her mom had always liked Sam. She'd been so disappointed in him when they broke up, so she'd urged Alli to get on with her life and not wait for Sam to come back.

Alli felt relieved that this conversation was over. Telling her mom she was going to be a grandmother could wait till after the wedding. There basically wasn't any other choice unless she decided to tell Sam and she simply didn't know how to do that right now. Everything had been going great, but she was still afraid he might walk away if he knew they were starting a family immediately.

CHAPTER 18

*S*am went online to see what he needed to do to apply for a Minnesota wedding license. It appeared they both were required to go in person to the court house. He wasn't sure if Las Vegas reported marriages to Minnesota, but from what he'd read online, it didn't appear they did. So, he decided it was best to not say anything unless it came up somehow from the state of Minnesota. Better to ask for forgiveness later, that is, if she ever found out. After all, it just really seemed like a moot point since they would simply end up being married twice.

He sent Alli a text to see if she could meet him at the court house in Shakopee after work on Thursday to apply for the marriage license. She replied immediately with yes. He was keeping his fingers crossed he wouldn't get anything in the mail from the State of Nevada before the wedding.

Sam waited outside the courthouse for Alli. He felt extremely agitated and he knew it was entirely nerves. So what if the clerk checked and said they were already married? The world wouldn't end. She might be a bit mad he hadn't told her, but it was ultimately what she wanted. And of course, just maybe, he could plead ignorance on his part?

Alli walked up to him, slipped her arms around his waist, and gave him a quick kiss on the lips. "Hello, Sam." A smile spread across her face as she took his hand in hers. "I've been waiting a long time for this. Let's do it."

Sam squeezed her hand. "Yes, you have."

The receptionist at the info desk pointed them down a hallway where they approached the clerk at the license window.

"We'd like to apply for a marriage license," Sam said.

"Certainly, you've come to the right place." The clerk handed them each a form on a clipboard with a pen. "You can take a seat to fill this out and bring it back up to me when you're done."

"Thanks," Sam said as they walked over to the sitting area to sit down.

When he got to the section where it asked if you had been married before, he hesitated for a second. Certainly, it didn't mean to the person you were marrying, so he checked the 'No' box. He continued on to the bottom where he signed his name and dated it.

Alli finished a couple of minutes later. "Ready, Sam?" she asked with excitement in her eyes.

"Definitely," he answered and stood up to follow her lead over to the clerk waiting at the window.

The clerk took the clipboards and removed the applications checking to be sure every question was answered along with their signatures, then paper clipped them together. "Looks good. I see your date is coming up soon, so I'll put the application in the urgent pile. You'll get a notice in the mail when it has been filed with the State."

"Thank you," Sam said.

"Thanks," Alli said as they turned to walk away.

"Want to have dinner at O'Brien's Pub?" he asked.

"Sounds great. I'll meet you over there." When they reached the parking lot, Alli turned toward Sam and kissed him with one of her kisses that would leave him wanting more, then walked in the direction of her car.

Damn, how he loved her. And she knew exactly how to turn him on, totally making him want to skip dinner and go back to the town-house. He could see her excitement to be finally getting married.

He pulled into the parking spot across from her and they walked into the restaurant. Usually, if you got there before five o'clock it was easy to get a table immediately. The hostess showed them to a table by the window and only minutes later the waitress showed up to get their drink order.

"So how was your day, Alli?" Sam asked.

"The best part was at the court house." She was smiling from ear to ear.

"I can tell," he said grinning, as her happiness was contagious.

"I've been waiting for this so long that I can't believe it's actually happening."

"Well, you can believe it. I think we signed our lives away."

Alli paused for a moment. "This is what you want, isn't it?"

"Sorry, that maybe didn't come out right. Alli, I can't imagine spending my life with anyone but you." He watched her face light up again. Lately, probably due to the wedding she completely had this glow about her. Whatever was causing it, he liked it.

"So what did you come up with for the honeymoon?"

"I figured since fate led us to both to be in Las Vegas at the same time and ultimately brought us back together, the only choice was Las Vegas."

"I agree wholeheartedly. Vegas it is!"

"Great! I took the liberty of booking us at the Bellagio, so I hope that hotel is okay with you?"

"Sounds perfect."

"I'll go ahead and get our air tickets booked. When do you want to fly out? The next day?"

"I'd like to open gifts the day after with our families and close friends. So let's leave on Monday."

"Okay and when do you want to come back? The following Sunday?"

"That sounds good. Maybe we can see a couple of shows and do some sightseeing like the Hoover Dam, too."

"You got it. I'll take care of everything."

"Thanks, Sam. Have I told you lately how much I love you?"

"Yes. But you can tell me that as often as you like. I love you, Alli. I'm sorry I was so stubborn, I missed you so much those six months we were apart."

The waitress arrived with their meals. O'Brien's Pub was known for their Irish fare dishes so Alli had ordered the Shepherd's Pie, while Sam ordered the Guinness Pot Roast.

After they finished eating Alli said, "I almost forgot to let you know that Susie is having a little get together at her place on Saturday night to introduce everyone to her new boyfriend, Trevor."

"The guy from Chicago that she met in Vegas?"

"Yes, I guess it has been working out well for them. She seems to really like him."

"Sounds like we have plans for Saturday night then. I look forward to meeting him." Sam couldn't help recalling how close he may have come to losing Alli to Trevor's friend that night in Vegas. She was his now, after all they were engaged, so he didn't have anything to worry about. He knew Alli loved him and he loved her, he just hoped this guy knew that and wasn't showing up at the party with his friend.

CHAPTER 19

Saturday morning, Alli woke up in bed lying next to Sam. Life was good.

"You awake, Babe?" Sam asked sliding his arm under her head and pulling her closer to him.

She turned and laid her head on his chest. "I see you're ready to go." She laughed, rolled on top of him, and gave him a big kiss, as the sheet slipped to the floor leaving their naked bodies uncovered. Before she knew it, he returned the kiss and quickly rolled her onto her back. Morning sex was always one of his favorites and Alli was always a willing partner, enjoying it equally.

After showering, they headed to the grocery store to pick up a veggie and fruit platter to bring to the party along with some wine. First though, they stopped to get a coffee and pastry for a quick breakfast.

About five o'clock, Alli headed out since she'd promised Susie she would arrive early to help set up for the party. "I'm leaving," she called out to Sam from the front door.

"See you at seven." Sam walked over to Alli and gave her a kiss that became a long kiss. He couldn't help noticing how hot she looked in her tight jeans and rust colored flannel shirt clinging to her curves perfectly.

~

ALLI CARRIED in her bags to Susie's condo. "Looks like you have everything under control. You obviously don't need my help."

Susie took the bags from Alli and set them on the counter. "I hope so. There's so many things to do at the last minute. Glad you're here."

"Is Trevor here yet?"

"No, he's watching the game at the bar with Dallas. They'll be here about quarter to seven."

"Dallas… you didn't tell me he was here."

"Didn't know he was coming until yesterday when they arrived at my place."

"Are they staying with you?"

"No, they got a hotel room down the road. Just felt like the right thing to do since we haven't known each other that long and haven't been together in person since Vegas."

"That's perfectly understandable. I get it."

"Am I being weird?" Susie asked.

"I don't think so."

"How did Trevor take it?"

"He said he understood. I'm kind of glad Dallas came with him, so he's not at the hotel alone, though."

"Did you tell Trevor that I'm engaged?" Alli asked.

"Yes, I told him last night."

"So Dallas knows then? I hope he didn't come along hoping to spend time with me."

"Trevor said Dallas really liked you, so I hope he told him," Susie stated reluctantly.

"You mean you don't know? He could possibly come in here thinking we could still be a thing?"

"Guess we'll simply have to wait and see what happens."

"I definitely hope it *happens* before Sam gets here."

"It'll be fine. You and Dallas didn't have sex or anything, so there's nothing for Sam to get mad about. Right?"

"No, we absolutely didn't have sex. Only a kiss. I wanted to see if there was anything there in case it didn't work out with Sam." Alli sat down on one of the bar stools.

"A kiss is just a kiss. Sam doesn't have to know and he won't, unless you tell him. I'm pretty sure Dallas isn't going to say anything. Guys don't kiss and tell. Do they?"

"Hell, if I know."

"Well, guess we'll basically have to wait and see what transpires. This is so *not* on me. You should've called Dallas back and told him you were engaged and it wasn't going to work out between the two of you."

"I know... Dallas is a nice guy and I just wanted to..."

"Keep your options open."

"Right. But I should've let him know after the engagement. I totally forgot about him with all the wedding plans and all. And, I never expected to see him again."

At quarter to seven, the doorbell rang. Susie opened the door where Trevor and Dallas stood waiting. She gave Trevor a big kiss and then welcomed them into the main room. Dallas immediately made eye contact with Alli who was standing behind the counter in the kitchen. The guys both carried in bags containing snacks and alcohol. They set them down, slowly removing the items and placing them on the counter with the other food that had already been set out.

Alli was at a loss for words. What did she say to this handsome man standing at the counter across from her? She could tell he was attracted to her when she looked into his eyes.

"Alli, it's good to see you. You look great. How have you been?" He walked around the counter to where she stood.

"Good. How about you?"

"When I heard Trevor was coming to Minneapolis to see Susie, I couldn't pass up the opportunity to see you again."

The doorbell rang and the door opened. Sam walked in just as Dallas leaned toward Alli and gave her a big hug.

He took her by surprise, so her hands went up against his chest. "Dallas, we need to talk. I need to tell you that I'm engaged." Alli backed away from him slightly and held her hand up with her engagement ring. "I'm sorry. I should've called you back and told you. We never really started a relationship, so I thought it didn't matter and I didn't think I'd ever see you again." She paused and could see the hurt in Dallas' eyes. "I'm sorry."

"Sorry for what?" Sam asked coming up behind Alli and wrapping his arms around her waist.

"You must be the lucky guy." Dallas stepped back and extended his hand to shake Sam's. "Congratulations. Anyone can tell she's one special lady."

Alli was freaking out inside. What was she to do? The only thing at this point was to introduce them. "Sam, this is Dallas. We met in Vegas. You might remember him from the Oasis Steak House restaurant. He's a friend of Trevor's."

"Dallas, nice to meet you," Sam said shaking his hand.

"Dallas, can I steal you away for a minute?" Susie walked over and took his arm to guide him into the other room, away from Alli.

Dallas reluctantly walked away, leaving Alli and Sam alone in the kitchen.

Alli turned to face Sam.

"What was that all about?" Sam asked searching Alli's face for answers.

"Nothing. There's nothing going on between me and Dallas."

"I'm trusting there isn't, but this isn't the place or time to discuss it. We'll talk about it later. Okay?"

"But, I just want to—"

"Later." Sam took her in his arms and kissed her as if he'd never let her go.

Alli was completely breathless when he finally ended the kiss. She noticed Dallas watching them out of the corner of her eye.

Sam and Alli walked into the main room, where everyone had

congregated, to greet their friends acting as if nothing had happened. Nothing *had* actually happened. Although, she sensed Sam was deeply aggravated by the scene he'd walked in on, but she had every confidence he wouldn't let on how upset he was to anyone. It would've been better to talk it out right now, instead of letting him stew about it, but he was right, it would be better done later. And in private.

CHAPTER 20

*A*lli couldn't wait for the night to end. Sam stayed close to her the entire evening and she caught Dallas staring at her more than a couple times.

"Do you want a glass of wine, Alli?" Sam asked.

"No, I'll just have a Raspberry Sprite. Don't want to drink and drive," she offered as an excuse for not drinking any wine. Soon, though, he would start to wonder about her sudden alcohol avoidance.

"Sure," Sam said and headed into the kitchen to get her a drink.

Susie momentarily took Sam's seat next to her. "Everything okay?"

"Not really, but I'll have to tell you later."

"You sure you're okay?"

"Yeah, I'll be fine."

Sam returned and handed Alli's drink to her as Susie excused herself and got up.

About midnight, Alli and Sam left the party. They'd come at different times so both their cars were there, which meant they would be driving home separately.

Once they were at Sam's townhouse, Alli walked in and sat down at the kitchen counter. She waited nervously while Sam used the bathroom.

He didn't take a seat next to her when he returned to the kitchen, but instead stood behind the counter now facing her.

She couldn't tell if he was simply tired, hurt or downright mad as hell.

"So, Dallas, huh." Sam locked eyes with her.

"It's nothing. We met them, him and his friends, while we were in Vegas, is all."

"He seemed quite friendly towards you, Alli."

"He called a few times after I got back home, but I didn't answer the calls."

"Did you *let* him *think* he had a chance with you?"

"After you left that morning, we still had a couple days in Vegas. We all, as a group, went to a show and dinner," Alli stated.

"I see."

"What was I supposed to do? Sit in the room alone? Tell Susie she couldn't go and had to stay with me?"

"That probably would've been a good plan, after we'd spent the night together."

"You left. I had no idea where we stood. Were we back together, or was it simply a great night of sex which it always was for us? Hell, I didn't even know if you would really call. You hadn't called me for over six months."

"I said I'd call you."

"None of this matters right now. You called. We're back together. Engaged."

"Did you sleep with him?" Sam asked.

"Really, that's where you want to go with this? No. Nothing happened with Dallas."

"You mean he didn't even kiss you or try to at least?"

"Okay, he kissed me. But that's it. I promise."

"Did you kiss him back?"

"Does it matter? I'm done talking about this. I never asked what you did while we were broken up since it doesn't matter because we weren't together at the time."

"That's the problem I'm having with this right now. I thought we'd gotten back together after having sex that night. I'm sorry I had to leave to catch my flight."

"You only said you'd call. I wasn't sure what that meant."

"Let me show you how I feel about us." Sam walked around the counter, wrapped his arms around Alli and kissed her. He took her hand and led her to the bedroom.

They undressed, practically ripping their clothes off each other all the while kissing like there was no tomorrow, quickly making it to the bed where Sam made passionate love to Alli, bringing them both the ecstasy they always enjoyed in each other's arms.

THEY FELL asleep with her head on his still bare chest, at least Alli did. Sam kept waking up during the night to make sure Alli was still there.

He finally got up to shower around seven the next morning and left Alli sleeping in the bed. Sam realized he wasn't so much angry with Alli as he was with himself. He should've never let their break-up go on for six months. He should've canceled his flight that morning and stayed in Vegas with her. Hell, they were married, only thing was she *didn't* know that.

Dallas, the guy she'd met in Vegas was definitely interested in Alli. There was no denying that. One could even say he was good-looking plus it was easy to tell he was educated and women would probably consider him a good catch. It also had become apparent he was a good guy, since he only kissed her and walked away. He knew Alli and he knew she didn't do one-night stands, so she'd probably told him that. Sadly, it was also obvious she'd wanted to keep her options open because she hadn't been sure he'd call her when she arrived back in Minneapolis. There was no way he could legitimately fault her for that.

A few minutes later, Alli opened the shower door and joined him.

He was the luckiest guy in the world to have a woman like her who obviously loved him. Damn it, he'd been such a fool. He kissed her and pulled her against him, sliding his hands over her wet and sleek sexy body.

Sam watched Alli finish dressing after they finished showering and moved behind her wrapping his arms around her waist. He bent his head down to nibble her ear. "I'm sorry I got mad about Dallas last night. I guess I was jealous."

Alli turned to face him. "You have nothing to worry about. I love you."

"I love you, so much, Alli." Sam kissed her and they finished dressing.

"What do you want to do today?" Alli asked.

"How about going out for brunch?"

"I'm starving. I'll go anywhere they're serving food." Alli put on her jacket, grabbed her purse, and followed Sam out to his car.

CHAPTER 21

*A*lli spent the next week concluding preparations for the wedding. Her mother would be arriving on Thursday to help Susie with the shower on Saturday afternoon. She and Sam had opted for a couples shower.

Thursday snuck up on her, and she was on her way to pick up her mother at the airport after leaving work. Hopefully, the plane was still on time.

Alli pulled up into the pick-up lane at the airport and saw her mother walk out the door. She got out to help with the suitcases, after first giving her mom a big hug. "Mom, so good to see you."

"You're looking good, Alli."

After stowing the suitcases in the back, they were on their way to her Aunt Gail's house.

"I see you brought a lot of luggage, Mom."

"I decided to stay through Christmas. Not much point in going home for a couple weeks since I'm already here. Your dad will fly in for the wedding, but he has to return for work and then he'll fly back for Christmas."

"That makes sense, I just didn't know this was the plan."

"Actually, only decided last weekend to change my return ticket. I have vacation time and since I'm only part time, I don't have to use that many days."

"I look forward to you being around till Christmas then." Alli's face lit up with a big smile.

Twenty minutes later, they pulled up to Aunt Gail's house. There was a lot of hugging and cheek kisses going on, but they managed to get the suitcases into the house.

"Congratulations, Alli, on finally getting that guy of yours to propose." Gail reached for her hand. "Let me take a look at the ring."

"I only saw a picture of it, I need to see it up close, too," her mother, Mary said.

"Oh, it's beautiful," Gail exclaimed. "Did you pick it out?"

"We'd looked at rings before we broke up and this is the one I'd picked back then."

"Well, you sure do look radiant. I think this engagement is exactly what you needed." Her mom hugged her.

"Well, I have to get going, it's getting late and I have to be up early for work in the morning. I'll call you tomorrow." Alli picked up her purse and coat.

"Okay, thanks for picking me up. Love you," Mary said.

HER MOM and Susie met up on Friday afternoon to finish up some plans for the shower. Luckily, Susie had taken the afternoon off since they still had quite a lot to do, according to her conversation with her mother. They'd both rejected any help from Alli because the shower was for her. Which was fine since lately, she'd been feeling a bit tired and wanted to be rested up for the shower. She knew it was her pregnancy causing it, but she didn't want anyone to notice anything different about her yet. Thankfully, she hadn't had any morning sickness yet, as that would be hard to explain. She rarely suffered from stomach issues or vomiting, so she had her fingers crossed. Hopefully, she would be one of the lucky ones who didn't get it. At least not, till after the wedding.

Sam had a lot going on at his company, Cavera Financial, so he'd been busy this week. He'd apologized and called her every night. He would be picking her up on Saturday, so they could go to the shower together. She was really looking forward to the wedding shower as she had waited a long time for this day to happen. This would be a special day for her.

CHAPTER 22

*M*innesota had been blessed with above normal temperatures during the week and this weekend it would be in the upper seventies. Alli was glad because that meant they could be outside for the shower, too. The theme they'd chosen was 'I Do BBQ'. Susie's condo development had a party room that included an outdoor patio area. It was perfect. Susie had taken her to see the room before she booked it. Since it was a couple's shower, they would be having games that included both the guys and girls.

Before she knew it, Saturday arrived. Alli dressed to impress today, she wanted everyone there to know what a lucky guy Sam was to be marrying her. Thankfully, she hadn't gained any weight yet, so her skin tight jeans still fit perfectly. Since it was a BBQ theme, she decided to wear her fancy brown and teal cowboy boots along with a teal and ivory plaid shirt loosely tucked in with a shiny gold belt. Her long blonde hair had been gently curled and framed her face with dangly gold looped earrings, adding their extra bling to her outfit.

A knock sounded on her apartment door.

"Alli, it's me," Sam said as he walked inside her apartment.

"I'll be right out," she answered.

An ivory fitted jean jacket, trimmed with brown accents

completed her outfit. After slipping it on, she glanced at the mirror just to be sure everything looked okay.

She turned to see Sam admiring her reflection in the full length mirror.

He came up behind her and wrapped his arms around her waist. "You look great, want to take a quick detour over to that bed, before we leave?"

She turned to face him and gave him a big sexy kiss. As their passion rose, she gently pushed at his chest and said, "I'd love to, but we'll be late. I'm counting on finishing this later though." Her face lit up with a huge smile for him.

"Okay." He gave her a kiss that totally left her wanting more. "We're definitely finishing this later!" He took her hand and led her to the front door before he changed his mind.

She reached over to the counter as they passed by and grabbed her purse. "I might need this." She laughed.

Quite a few people had already arrived, by the time they walked into Susie's party room. Kally, Jennifer and her mom were busy helping Susie with last minute preparations and she saw Kevin, Dustin and Tyler outside setting up the bean bag toss game.

Sam's parents, John and Gina Cavera arrived shortly after them. Due to their busy schedules as owners of Cavera Financial, which was the family owned business. Sam also worked there, but she hadn't seen them since she and Sam had gotten engaged. It felt a bit awkward.

Sam took her hand as they walked over to greet them.

Gina smiled and gave Alli a big hug. "Congratulations. I'm glad you both resolved everything because you two are definitely better together than apart."

"Thanks, Mom," Sam said and gave her a hug.

John shook her hand and gave her a quick hug. "Congratulations. Thanks for taking Sam off our hands." He had a huge smirk on his face and gave Sam a pat on the back, as guys are prone to do.

"Thanks, Dad." Sam rolled his eyes as he grinned.

Minutes later, Susie pulled Alli away with some last minute questions and Sam headed outside to see the guys.

Soon, the large room was filled with their friends and relatives which included cousins, aunts and uncles. One table was filled with gifts and another was decorated with wedding items and scrumptious looking food. They'd opted for a cupcake cake which was actually five tiers of cupcakes with five different flavors, Carrot, Lemon, Almond, Chocolate and Red Velvet, representing the autumn colors of Minnesota. It was beautiful.

"Susie, I love it! These cupcakes are incredible. Thanks for doing this," Alli said hugging Susie.

"You're my best friend. So of course, I'd do this for you!"

"I know, but it really was short notice."

"Well, that it was, but you know me, there isn't anything I can't do or get done if I set my mind to it."

"I do know that." Alli gave her a huge smile.

"Well, I think we should set the hot food out and get everyone in line to eat."

Quickly and like clockwork Susie, Kally, and Jennifer filled the table with the hot barbeque pork ribs and pulled pork. They pulled the cold salads from the fridge and set them out.

"Should I get Sam?"

"Yes, I want you two to be first in line, of course."

Alli walked outside to get Sam. She noticed the Bean Bag Toss game had been personalized with her and Sam's name along with their wedding date. Susie was amazing, how she managed this on such a short time frame, she had no idea.

"Sam, look these have our names and the date on them." She felt so lucky to have Susie as a friend! Feelings overwhelmed her and she almost started to tear up. She wasn't exactly sure why, since she usually wasn't that emotional. But she had read women could get overly emotional when pregnant due to hormone overload. She took Sam's hand and turned away, so he couldn't see her face. "We need to start the food line."

They filled their plates with all the delectable food items then sat down at a high bar table to eat. Alli looked around the room at all her friends and relatives who'd managed to clear their calendars to show up for this very short notice wedding shower. Her heart was completely overflowing with gratitude for each and every one of them showing up today.

"You look happy," Sam said.

"I am ecstatic actually that this day has finally arrived. Thank you for making it possible."

He leaned across and kissed her. "I love you, Alli. Sorry, I was such a jerk about everything. I'm so glad to be here with you today."

"I love you, too."

After everyone finished eating, Alli and Sam moved to the special chairs decorated for the bride and groom. There was a balloon arch over them which consisted of many satiny balloons in the various autumn colors, all tied together to form an arch effect.

Games were next on the agenda. These were not your old games from her mother's generation, but new and different ones for the younger generations. One of the games involved questions about her and Sam. They were to fill out the answers together first, then give them to Susie. Next, everyone filled out their answers to see if they could come up with the same answers Sam and Alli had written down.

One question was a bit tricky, however. *'How long have they been dating?'* She was sure it wasn't intentional to include this particular question, but felt obliged to put down the correct answer which meant not including the six months they'd been broken up. The break up hadn't been broadcast or anything like that, so some of her relatives she didn't see very often wouldn't have known about it. *'How many children do they want?'* She sincerely hoped everyone at least put down one considering they had one on the way, only no one knew except for her and Susie. Thankfully, Susie had everyone put their names on the sheets and hand them in, so Kally and Jennifer could tally them instead of going over them out loud.

Finally, it was time for opening presents. Dustin handed the gifts to Sam, who handed the card to Alli, who then handed it to Susie to put down on her list while Sam helped Alli unwrap the gifts. It was a pretty smooth operation and quick. Their friends were extremely generous and they received quite a few of the items on their gift registry.

After the last gift was opened, people migrated outside to play the bean bag toss game and chat. Beer, wine and punch continued to be served. She'd of course opted for the punch which was non-alcoholic. Not really being a big drinker normally, she hoped Sam wouldn't notice.

It had been a great day in Alli's book, she couldn't have asked for a better Wedding Shower. By the time they arrived back at Alli's apartment, she was feeling a bit tired. Sam wasn't waiting to finish what they'd started earlier, though.

He took her in his arms and began showering her with kisses. She was swept along as the chemistry between them led to full blown passion and found them in the bedroom, undressing as quickly as they could. Within minutes, they were on the bed kissing, wrapped in each other's arms. "I've been waiting all day to finish what we started. You're so beautiful, Alli."

She smiled and rolled on top of him. "Glad to oblige."

CHAPTER 23

With less than three weeks until the wedding, this Friday was the appointment at the bridal shop for last minute alterations on her dress and her mother had yet to purchase a dress for herself. Hopefully, they would find one at the shop or her mom and Aunt Gail would be spending the next week dress shopping. At this point, it was most likely too late to order a dress and have it altered, so Alli really hoped they'd find one her mother liked today.

Alli was the first to arrive at the Bridal Shop. Soon Susie, Kally and Jennifer arrived together. It hadn't appeared their dresses would need much altering, going by the measurements, except on the hems possibly. A few minutes later, her mom and Aunt Gail walked in. Alli already was in the fitting room changing into her wedding dress so they began looking through the mother of the bride racks for a dress.

Alli heard a knock on the fitting room door.

"Need any help?" Susie asked.

"Sure come on in," Alli answered.

Susie came in shutting the door behind her. She immediately picked up one side of the dress and helped Alli set it on the floor. Alli carefully stepped into the center opening right as the bridal store attendant came in to help. Together, they pulled the dress up so Alli could get it into position to be zipped up. The wedding dress was a strapless corset style fitted to just below the waist with a V-shape and then flared out with a slightly gathered skirt in ivory satin. Thankfully, it had been slightly loose in the bust when she bought it, realizing she'd need to have it taken in, but now due to her breasts being fuller, it was fine. The waist still fit nicely since she hadn't actually gained any weight, yet.

"Ready to go out to the large mirrors?" the attendant asked.

"Let's do it," Alli said and turned toward the door.

Susie and the attendant picked up the train which they would attach to the dress in the mirror room. Alli picked up the front of the dress skirt as she walked out to where her mother, Aunt Gail, Kally and Jennifer were waiting.

After the train was attached, Alli stared at herself in the large triple mirrors. She could hardly believe the image she saw was really her. She'd waited so many years for her wedding day and now it was only a couple of weeks away. Thankfully, the woman staring back at her didn't look pregnant but instead looked radiant.

"Alli, you look absolutely stunning!" her mother exclaimed with a huge smile for her daughter.

"You look beautiful, Alli," Susie said.

Aunt Gail, Kally and Jennifer voiced their agreement, also.

Alli turned from side to side to take in all the different angles of the dress. She hoped Sam would like it and think she looked beautiful, too.

"Sam will love it," Susie said as if she could read Alli's thoughts.

Alli smiled at Susie. "Thanks. I hope so."

The attendant brought out veils to try on and she picked one to be pinned into the back of her head where her hair would be piled into curls. She'd picked out her shoes earlier with only two inch heels, so she could walk around comfortably the whole night.

The dress fit perfectly so no alterations were needed, it would be kept at the store though, and she would pick it up the week of the wedding. Alli undressed and after she was back in her jeans and shirt, she met everyone at the mirror room where the bridesmaid dresses were being tried on. Her mother found a few options and was busy trying them on at the same time.

The bridesmaids' dresses arrived and only needed a few minor alterations that would be ready the following week. Her mother found a light yellow gold sleeveless fitted long dress with a scoop neckline and back slit that had a matching long sleeved jacked with a one hook closure in front. This dress only required a couple of alterations also and would totally compliment the rust bridesmaid dresses, bringing out the fall theme colors of the wedding.

"Well, good job, girls! I'd like to treat everyone to dinner at Porter's Steak House," her mother offered.

Alli grinned at her. "Thanks, Mom. I'm starving. Let's meet over there since we have multiple cars here."

They promptly left and met at the restaurant. It would be nice to have dinner with only the girls, she thought. Sam asked earlier if she wanted to have dinner, so she called to let him know there was a change of plans.

"So, how did your dress day go?" Sam asked after he answered her call.

"Great. It fit fine, found a veil and my mom found a dress. Oh and the bridesmaid dresses came in and only needed a few minor alterations."

"Sounds like you had a good day."

"My mom wants to take all of us girls to dinner at Porter's Steak House, will you be okay on your own for dinner?"

"Of course, go ahead and have a good time. I'm still at work so I'll pick something up to eat on the way home. Are you still stopping over later tonight?"

"Yes, I'll be there after we're done with dinner."

"Okay, see you later," Sam said.

Alli pulled into the parking lot to the restaurant a few minutes later. She was the last to arrive, so as soon as she walked in, the hostess came over to seat them at a table for six.

Everyone ordered steaks of course, since it was a steak house. And wine was ordered. This was getting tougher every time, she thought.

She'd ordered a glass of red wine, not knowing what else to do. She simply wouldn't drink it, of course.

Susie looked her way wondering what the heck she was doing ordering wine.

Maybe she'd plead the *'wine gives me a headache sometimes'* as a reason. After the waiter left the table, she excused herself to use the restroom. On her way, she looked for their waiter. "Do you serve non-alcoholic wine?"

"Yes, we do," he answered.

"Could you please change mine to a red non-alcoholic?"

"Sure."

"Please don't say anything about it being non-alcoholic when you serve the wine."

"Not a problem." He walked away.

Alli continued on to the restroom.

She wasn't sure if non-alcoholic wine tasted any good, but this way she wouldn't have to try to explain why she wasn't drinking tonight.

The wine was served without a problem. Bread and salads came out shortly afterwards.

Around seven, they left the restaurant and she was on her way to Sam's townhouse. It had been nice to hang out with her mom, Aunt Gail and her best friends, but she couldn't wait to see Sam. A girls night out was exactly what she'd needed, though. She pulled into the townhouse garage and closed the door. As soon as she walked inside, she was met with a big kiss from Sam.

"Did you have a nice time?" he asked.

"It really was nice. I don't get to see my mom that often or my Aunt Gail. All in all, it was a very enjoyable girl's night out with dinner."

The doorbell rang and she glanced toward the door.

"Must be my pizza." Sam walked to the door and opened it.

Alli had a clear view of the door now that she'd walked into the hallway. Her mouth dropped open. At the door stood a very pretty woman with long black hair holding open her long trench coat to reveal the sexy black lingerie she was wearing underneath it, which was really next to nothing at all. Spiked black heels totally added to the image she was trying to portray.

Sam apparently was speechless, as he hadn't said anything, yet.

The woman had obviously seen Alli behind Sam and immediately, closed her coat and tied the belt. "I'm so sorry," she said looking at Sam and then to Alli.

SAM LOOKED BACK AT ALLI. "Can you give us a minute?" He then stepped outside and closed the door behind him.

"Tori, what are you doing?" he asked.

"I think that's pretty obvious. Why didn't you tell me you had a girlfriend?" she asked.

"That is Alli and we are back together. I told you I wasn't ready to start dating again."

"I know but I just wanted to give you a push."

"I have loved Alli for a long time. And actually we're now engaged." He paused. "Tori, nothing personal but you simply aren't what I'm looking for."

"I'm so sorry. Sorry, I put you in this position."

The door behind him opened. Alli stood quietly, waiting in the doorway.

"Alli, this is Tori," Sam stated. "We went out once a few weeks before my birthday. She wasn't you, so I never called her again. She apparently thought this might make me want a second date."

"I'm so embarrassed. I had no idea he was—you are engaged. I'm leaving right now. Congratulations." With that Tori turned, walked away, got in her car and left.

Sam turned around and went inside with Alli. "I'm so sorry this happened. Are you okay, Alli?"

"Did you have sex with her?"

"Absolutely not."

"Why not? She looked pretty sexy, standing there in her lingerie."

"Because she's not you, Alli." He pulled her against his chest and kissed her.

Alli leaned back. "Did you kiss her?"

"Yes." Silence permeated the room. "It wasn't the same, though. The chemistry wasn't there. I think it was then, I knew for sure that you were the only one I wanted."

"But you still didn't call me." Alli backed a step away from him.

"I was working up my courage to call you because I knew how badly I'd screwed up. Hell, I hadn't heard from you, so I didn't know if you were dating anyone else. We were busy at work and I had the trip planned to Vegas. So I figured I'd call you when I got back." Sam closed the space between them and began sprinkling her face with kisses. "Alli, I love you so much."

Just then, the doorbell rang. *Again.*

Sam opened the door and was handed his pizza. "Thanks," he said. Immediately, he set the box on the kitchen counter and walked back to Alli. "Now, where were we?" He gave her his wickedly sexy grin.

Alli took his hand and led him to the bedroom. "Show me." She released his hand and slowly began taking her clothes off piece by piece to tantalize him with her sexy still trim body.

Abruptly, she stopped as her jeans slid to the floor. "Oh, did you need to eat your pizza first?"

"Not a chance in hell I would pick a pizza over you!" He began stripping his clothes off in a hurry. "Besides, I've always enjoyed cold pizza."

Seconds later, they hit the smooth sheets with their now naked bodies.

CHAPTER 24

The following Saturday was the bachelorette party. Alli dressed in her skin tight jeans and a low cut black sparkly knit top, after applying her make-up and curling her hair. Next, red and gold dangly earrings, a red bold necklace resting slightly above her cleavage and a red and gold bracelet completed her clubbing look.

Her breasts appeared a bit larger due to the pregnancy. She could tell but Sam hadn't mentioned anything yet. Which was good, wasn't it? The dilemma was whether she should tell him before or after the wedding. If she hadn't gone in to get the birth control prescription, she wouldn't have known so soon.

She was so afraid to tell him, which was the problem. Because what if he got mad and called off the wedding? A huge part of her kept saying he wouldn't do that, but what if he did? Either way, she would still be pregnant and having a baby. *His baby.* Maybe if the right opportunity came along she would tell him but unfortunately, it hadn't. *What would it hurt to wait, anyway?*

After the incident with Tori showing up at Sam's door, she'd really been scared of losing him again. He'd told her nothing happened between him and Tori, so she believed him. The whole six months they'd been split up, she'd tried desperately not to think about Sam being with someone else. For the most part, she'd succeeded, but when she saw Tori, she realized how easily it would have been for him to be with someone else. Heck, she'd purposely not dated because she was still in love with Sam, but after meeting Dallas she'd realized that meeting and liking someone else was entirely possible. Loving them, however, would take time. A lot of time.

The doorbell rang. "Come on in, it's open," Alli yelled.

Susie walked into the living room, as Alli came out of the bedroom carrying a pair of black heeled boots and a small black shoulder strap purse.

"Lookin' good for a pregnant lady!" Susie commented.

"Does that mean I look pregnant?" Alli asked.

"Hell, no. No one would guess there is a little, tiny baby in there," Susie said pointing to Alli's stomach.

"Thank heavens!"

"You ready to go?"

Alli slipped on her boots, then a fitted sateen jacket. "Yup."

"You okay?" Susie asked as she watched the smile fade from Alli's face.

"How am I going to work this no alcohol thing into a bachelorette party?"

"I've been thinking about that, actually. I think you should simply order virgin Pina Coladas. That way they totally look like a real drink but it's just fruit basically and will be good for the baby. Let me order for you at the bar or I'll talk to the waiter privately."

"Okay. That makes me feel better." Alli's smile returned. "So where are we going? I never did ask."

"Crooners in Minneapolis. Not a club like we're used to, but I thought you could maybe use something a bit calmer. It's an old school Jazz type supper club. They feature live bands, a dance floor and great food, I hear."

"I think I've heard of it. It's kind of new isn't it?"

"Yeah, only been open a couple of years now. Tonight, they have a tribute band to the 'Ladies of the 80's'. Mariah Carey, Christina Aguilera, Brittany Spears, Beyonce and Madonna. Should be good."

"Sounds perfect." Alli smiled. "Didn't think I was quite up to actual clubbing since I can't drink. Who all is coming?"

"Kally, Jennifer, your mom and aunt, Sam's mom, a couple of your cousins—about twenty in all."

"Any idea where the guys are going?"

"You're asking me? Didn't you ask Sam?"

"No. Didn't want Sam to think I was keeping tabs on him, especially after the Tori incident."

Susie began laughing hysterically. "I absolutely crack up every time I try to visualize a naked woman at Sam's door."

"Yeah well, it makes a person wonder what goes on when you're not around. But, just for the record, she wasn't totally naked."

"Almost! You guys were broke up when he met her. Sam would never cheat on you, now that you're back together."

"I know, but still. It was a very awkward moment."

"But the make-up sex was awesome you said."

"Let's get going. I'm anxious to see this place." Alli couldn't help smiling about the make-up sex.

Thirty minutes later, they pulled into the large parking lot, bordering Moore Lake. A reserved table for twenty people was near the stage, so they'd have a clear view of the singers. Their reservation was for six o'clock, so they'd have time to eat before the show started at seven-thirty.

Kally and Jennifer walked in with a rust, gold and brown balloon bouquet trailing behind them. Jennifer walked over to Alli to place a Bride-to-Be ribbon sash, like the Miss America ones, on her.

"Thanks." Alli straightened the sash as she spotted her mom and aunt walking over to the table.

"You look good, Alli," her mom said and hugged her.

Everyone then became enthralled in the various conversations going on around the table.

Susie handed her a Pina Colada which she assumed was non-alcoholic.

"Thanks," Alli said as she took a quick sip to be sure there wasn't any alcohol in it and gave Susie a thumbs-up gesture. She picked up a menu as the waiter arrived to take their orders. "Walleye sounds good," she said.

The waiter then continued to make his way around the table.

Promptly at seven-thirty, the band and singers took the stage. They urged the customers to take advantage of the dance floor, especially the bachelorette party who knew all the songs and sang along with the singers. It didn't take much urging from the crowd to get the Bride-to Be and her friends out dancing. Soon the dance floor was full with everyone having a great time showing off their dance moves.

After the last set ended, around eleven o'clock, the ladies exited the restaurant. Those who had chosen to drink called an Uber, so they wouldn't be driving while under the influence.

Alli drove since she hadn't been drinking.

"So did you have a good time?" Susie asked.

"Definitely. You know I love to go dancing and the food was great. Thanks for planning it."

"Well, hope the guys had a good time tonight," Susie commented.

"Yeah and didn't get into any trouble!"

Alli and Susie burst out laughing.

"Like that guy you were dancing with?"

"What guy? That was an old man!" Alli tried to keep a straight face.

"But a damn good looking silver fox and he was hot for you Alli!"

"And thanks for asking the crowd for a man to dance with the Bride-to-Be!"

"Whatever!" Susie exclaimed.

They both continued laughing even though they were trying their best not to.

CHAPTER 25

Sam wasn't sure why he'd spent the day worrying about Alli's upcoming bachelorette party, but he had. He trusted her completely, only the incident with the guy, Dallas, from Vegas, made him realize how stupid he'd been to break up with Alli, the woman he loved so much that it hurt to even think about her with another guy.

These parties were for the bride and groom to have a last night of freedom before signing their lives away forever. Which by the way, he was more than happy to sign their marriage certificate. There were always stories making the rounds of bride and grooms-to-be having that last fling or more correctly stated should be having sex with someone else since it would no longer be an option after the wedding.

He'd pretty much ordered Dustin to keep it simple tonight. He didn't want any cakes with a woman jumping out or strippers showing up and he'd made Dustin swear neither of those things would be happening. So instead of those options, they were having a poker party at Dustin's parent's house on Lake Minnetonka.

This was a casual party, so he put on jeans, a brown plaid shirt and a pair of brown loafer style shoes. He was so tempted to call Alli, but figured it would look like he was checking up on her, so he didn't.

Dustin's dad was the president of Minnetonka State Bank and

their house was really a mansion located on Lake Minnetonka. He'd spent a lot of time there while growing up since he and Dustin had been best friends since grade school. Sam's parent's house was large, too, but they lived on Christmas Lake, also in Minnetonka, only a few minutes away from Dustin's family home. The nice thing about Dustin's parent's home was they had a rather large guest house, where Dustin had lived throughout all the summer vacations during college and still kept some things there. This was where the bachelor party would be held.

Sam pulled up and parked in the separate driveway it had from the main house.

Dustin came out to greet him, "Well, this is it, one of your last days of being a free man, Sam."

"Awe, come on. You know how I feel about Alli. She's the best thing that ever happened to me."

Dustin nodded. "Yeah, I know." He paused to look out at the lake. "I always loved the way the lake looks bordered in the Fall colors."

They both paused a few moments to take in the gorgeous view and then went inside.

The guest house had its own game room complete with a poker table, foosball table, pool table and a big screen TV. Outside on the patio, the large eight person hot tub was uncovered and bubbling like crazy.

Sam hadn't thought about bringing swim trunks but he knew Dustin's mom kept a whole drawer full in the mud room for those unplanned hot tub parties. Women's swim suits were in a different drawer. It was a nice night, so it might be enjoyable to take advantage of the soothing water with a great view of the lake.

Soon the guys began arriving. There were about twenty-five that showed up, mostly old high school and college friends. Sam grabbed a beer along with a few snacks to nibble on then sat down at the poker table with five of the guys to play poker. Only chips were allowed as they'd decided not to play for money. He was an above average poker player and didn't want to take anyone's money. That wasn't what it was about for him, he liked playing and winning, but it wasn't about the money. Nearly an hour later, he walked away with his large stack of chips to try a different game.

The doorbell rang and Dustin opened the door to let in the pizza delivery guy, carrying in a stack of pizzas and wings boxes. Dustin had ordered a lot of food so the guy needed to make a few trips to carry everything in. After he left, the guys swarmed to the counter to fill their plates with pizza slices, wings, and sauce dips.

Some of the guys joked about dessert when they were done and where was the cake.

"It's coming. Patience my friends," Dustin told them all.

Sam gave Dustin a look that meant *it better not be what it sounded like.*

Dustin walked over to Sam. "No girl in the cake. I promised."

"Better not be." Sam headed over to the pool table, pulling Dustin with him.

They played another team and kept winning. About ten, Sam, decided to try out the hot tub. After he finished changing, the doorbell rang again. He felt every muscle in his body tense. He was pissed to say the least. Who would be at the door, ringing the bell at this time? Dustin went to the door and then stepped outside closing the door behind him. Damn! Sam decided to take care of this before it started, so he opened the door and stepped outside to find Dustin talking to a beautiful woman, holding a couple of large bakery boxes. Her back was to him, so he couldn't see her face. When she turned around, he was shocked to see Deanna, who seemed to be even more stunning than in high school and college.

"Sam, I heard you were going to be out of circulation permanently, so I decided to stop by." She handed the boxes to Dustin and walked over to give Sam a big hug.

"Deanna, it's been a long time."

"About ten years. Too bad, you could never get past the fact that I was Dustin's little sister."

"We gave it shot back in college."

"Exactly what I said, you couldn't get past who I was, even though I'd had a crush on you since grade school."

"I'm sorry. I never realized..." Sam stared at Deanna.

"I know. Guess the chemistry simply wasn't there or you would have pursued me."

"I'm sorry." Sam didn't know what else to say. He'd never realized she liked him all those years ago. She was four years younger than them, so she was always way behind them in school. By the time she'd really caught up with them, he'd moved on and then he met Alli.

"That's okay. I'm glad you found someone who makes you happy. I just stopped over to see mom and she told me about the bachelor party going on down at the guest house. So, I thought I'd stop down and say hi since it was obviously too late to order a cake to jump out of." She laughed and looked toward Dustin. "Mom said she was supposed to bring the desserts down about ten so here I am."

Sam smiled at her. "Thanks. It was good to see you again."

"Congratulations and best of luck on your marriage to Alli." She leaned in to hug him again and then turned to walk back up the driveway to the main house.

Sam took one of the boxes from Dustin.

He'd just stood silently observing Sam's exchange with Deanna. "Sorry, man. Didn't know my little sis was stopping by."

"Did you know she had a crush on me all those years we were in school?"

"She never really told me, but she always asked about you come to think of it. And she always managed to be around under our feet when you were over here, if you remember back then."

"I think I always thought of her as your little sis and never as girl-friend material. Sorry, if she thought I led her on. We only went on two dates and it simply didn't feel right, so that was it. Sorry."

"No need to be sorry." Dustin shrugged. "She has a boyfriend currently anyway, so not sure why she wanted to confess her feelings now."

"I am very glad there wasn't a cake with a girl jumping out. What's in these boxes?"

"Mom had the bakery make us those special cream cheese brownies, dark chocolate brownies, carrot bars and lemon bars that she used to make for us when we were kids. She said we would need dessert."

"I love all of those bars. Do we have to share with the guys?"

"I think so, cuz there is really a lot of them in here. We could never eat them all, even if we tried."

They laughed as they walked back into the guest house and put the boxes on the counter. Quickly, they grabbed one of each for their own plates before everyone else practically stampeded up to the bar for the dessert treats. Sam relished the bars as they were delicious and tasted exactly like he remembered.

"I see you have swim trunks on. I'll change and join you out there." Dustin headed to the mudroom.

Sam grabbed a towel and made his way to the patio. The outside lights were off with only the hot tub lights on, so you could see the lake. Along with all the stars filling the clear sky on this November night. No one else was in the tub, probably because they'd all gone in for dessert. He slid in slowly, embracing the warm water of the whirlpool jets on his back. The lights from the houses on the opposite shoreline of the lake sparkled in the night. He missed being on the lake after growing up on one. During the past six months, he'd been looking at lakeshore properties and recently found one he liked. He hadn't made an offer yet because he was waiting to show it to Alli first.

"Here," Dustin said and handed Sam a beer.

"Thanks. I really miss being on the lake. I'm thinking about buying a lakeshore property."

"Every time I'm out here, I think the same thing. I love living in the downtown area but I really feel I'm home when I'm here. Have you talked to Alli about it?"

"Not yet. I will after the wedding."

"Since Deanna was being honest about how she felt, I want to mention that I've liked Susie ever since I met her."

"Really?"

"Yeah, never seemed like she was interested in me though, so I didn't pursue it."

"Wow! I never would've guessed. Do you want me to say something to Alli about it?"

"No. She's dating that guy from Chicago right now. Probably lost my chance."

Sam changed the subject, "I love sitting out here at night looking out over the lake."

"Me, too."

"I think I'm over my beer limit. May have to sleep over tonight, if that's okay with you?" Sam asked.

"Of course. Not a chance I'm letting my best friend drive when he's been drinking."

They both slid down so their shoulders were under water and sat silently gazing out over the lake at the sky full of stars until the quiet was broken by more guys joining them along with many drunken conversations.

Sam guessed they would all be spending the night in Dustin's guest house.

CHAPTER 26

The following week, Alli took Thursday and Friday off work, so she could be sure to get everything taken care of for the wedding. Probably was a good idea since she hadn't really been able to concentrate on work the past few days anyway. It was already Wednesday and she was meeting Sam after work for dinner at Whiskey Inferno to go over all her lists to make sure they hadn't forgotten anything. She planned to spend the night at Sam's since they hadn't seen each other since Sunday when they'd gone to brunch with his parents at Maynard's on Lake Minnetonka. They'd discussed the bachelor and bachelorette parties briefly and then moved on to discussing the wedding.

Alli walked into the restaurant lobby where Sam was waiting for her.

He gave her a big kiss.

"Wow. What did I do to deserve that?" Alli asked with a huge smile on her face.

"You agreed to be my wife." It was obvious he was in a good mood.

"Okay. Not sure what's gotten into you, but I like it." Alli gave him a quick kiss. The waiting room wasn't full, but she knew people were watching them.

Saved by the hostess, they were led to a booth.

"Alli, do you want a glass of wine?" Sam asked when he saw the waiter approaching.

"No, I have a slight headache, so I'll just have a Coke. You know wine gives me a headache sometime." This was getting ridiculous, she needed to tell him. Now that the wedding was only a few days away though, it definitely seemed like a better conversation for the honeymoon. She didn't want anything to go wrong. Her baby needed a father.

After dinner, they watched TV at Sam's place for a short time before they found themselves in the bedroom, having crazy passionate sex. She knew it was partly because of the thought of losing Sam to Tori had scared her immensely and the love she felt for him seemed to be at a new level since she'd became pregnant. Sam seemed different too, but she didn't know why, but she liked it. *Every single minute of the love, he was showering her with.*

In the morning, Sam apologized for having to run into the office for a couple of hours.

After he left, she showered and dressed. She decided to use his computer to check her emails and print out her updated to do list for the wedding. She noticed a folder on his desk labeled marriage license. What possessed her to open it, she had no idea. Inside was a Las Vegas Marriage Certificate. She picked it up. It was dated June 30 and had both their names on it, along with a bright gold State of Nevada seal stamped on the corner.

Alli leaned back in the chair still holding the certificate. She tried to focus on that night. They'd left the group and made their way down the strip. She now remembered the Wedding Chapel where they'd stopped in, thinking it would be fun to pretend to get married. All this time, she'd thought these places weren't real. Although, now that she thought about it, it could've been real. When she woke up in his hotel room the following morning, his bag was already packed, so he must've taken it with him.

"Damn him!" They were already married and he hadn't bothered to mention it to her. *He knew.*

She didn't even need the wedding now, but she sure as hell wanted it. A big wedding had always been her dream. Was this why he proposed to her? Because they were already married? Maybe he still didn't want to get married, only felt trapped after their spur of the moment decision in Vegas? But did it even matter? She knew he loved her and he'd made a point of showing her ever since they got back from Vegas.

The biggest question was would he want the baby?

Alli put the certificate back in the folder and placed it exactly where she found it. After printing her list, she texted Susie to meet her for lunch. She had to tell someone.

Susie was waiting for her at Panera.

Alli ordered at the counter and took a seat in the booth across from Susie.

A panicked look crossed Susie's face. "Is everything okay?"

"No." Alli began fidgeting with her hands on the table. "He lied to me."

"Lied? About what?"

"Well, apparently that night in Vegas when we got back together, we stopped at a Wedding Chapel and got married."

"Oh." Susie looked shocked.

"Why didn't he tell me?" The tears welling in Alli's eyes broke free and ran down her cheeks.

Susie got up and moved to sit next to Alli putting her arm around her. "It's going to be okay. So what if you're already married? This way, you get the big wedding on Saturday. That's what you wanted."

"I know. But it's not a good way to start a marriage out by lying."

"Did you tell him about the baby?"

"No. It never seemed like the right time."

"So does that mean you're lying to him?"

"I simply haven't told him yet. That's not lying. Is it?"

"Maybe he hasn't found the right way or time to tell you about Vegas either?"

"Do you think I'm overreacting?"

"I think both of these issues will most likely be resolved in a couple of days."

"So, you think we should go on with the wedding as planned?"

"Of course! There's no reason not to. You both love each other, don't you?"

"Yes."

"He proposed didn't he?"

"Yes."

"Then we're having a wedding on Saturday. It's going to be beautiful. You're going to be a beautiful bride."

"So, you don't think I should tell him I know we're already married?"

"I think that conversation and the baby can be discussed on the honeymoon. Neither conversation will change the fact that you're already married and that you're pregnant, so I say wait until you get to Vegas."

"Okay." Alli let out a huge sigh. "That makes me feel better and makes total sense. Let's eat."

They got up and walked to the pick-up window to get their lunches.

CHAPTER 27

*A*lli felt nervous about seeing Sam tonight at the church and rehearsal dinner. She was the world's worst liar, everyone could always tell if she wasn't telling the truth. He would probably be able to tell she'd seen the file merely by looking at her. However, if he didn't confront her by asking she wouldn't have to lie, so he wouldn't know. All she had to do was smile and avoid any talk about marriage licenses. She was sure she could manage that.

Why couldn't she simply decide on which dress to wear? She'd already looked at every dress in her closet and at this very moment, she didn't like any of them. Finally, she pulled out a chocolate brown and gold leopard print long sleeved dress with a deep V-neck that fell barely above her knees. After slipping it on, she took a peek in the mirror and liked what she saw. Thank heavens, it still fit. Her dark brown heels would go with it perfectly, so she slipped them on and selected her dark brown, small evening size purse to complete the ensemble.

Susie was stopping by to pick her up, so she could ride home later tonight with Sam. Promptly at five-thirty, she heard a car horn honking in her driveway and walked over to the window to see if it was Susie. It was, so she put on a black full length wool coat then picked up her purse and a black tote bag, with her wedding notes all in a pretty gold binder neatly tucked inside it.

"How's it going?" Susie asked.

"Good, I guess. Just nervous about seeing Sam."

"Sam? Why on earth would you be nervous?"

"I'm afraid he'll know I saw the folder," Alli confessed.

"You totally get that out of your head right now. There's no way he'd know that."

"I know, but I keep thinking what if?"

"It's completely irrelevant at this point, anyway. Now the baby is another story, but he'll know in a couple of days and he loves you Alli, so everything is going to work out fine. Let's go have a good time."

Alli relaxed a little. "Okay, okay! I'm excited to see my dad."

Twenty minutes later, they pulled up at St. Paul's Lutheran Church. She saw Sam's car already in the parking lot, and her parents were just entering the church.

Susie parked and they walked inside.

Sam was waiting by the door to give her a big kiss as soon as she stepped inside the church. "How was your day?" he asked smiling at her.

"Good. Are you ready for this?" she asked.

"Looking forward to spending every day with you, Alli, from now on."

Her eyes began watering because she was so happy to hear him say that. She didn't think she'd ever get tired of him saying such sweet things to her.

"Are you okay, Alli?" he asked putting his arm around her.

"I'm fine. I'm completely happy," she answered and smiled.

He took her hand and they walked into the foyer where her parents, his parents, the bridal party, and the pastor were waiting for them.

She walked over to her dad and gave him a big hug. "So glad you're here, Daddy."

He hugged her back. "Wouldn't miss this for anything. This is an important day for my baby girl."

The pastor made his way to the front of the church and tapped the microphone to see if it was working. "If everyone could take a seat, I'll go over the service order, where everyone needs to be and when they need to be there."

They all took seats and the pastor began giving directions. When he was done, it was practice time, so Alli headed to the back of the church with her dad, the bridesmaids, and groomsmen. Sam, his parents and her mother stayed at the front of the church. It was pretty much the usual wedding order and procession style. The singer was there along with the pianist for the music portion. Everything went well and they were done within an hour.

Alli rode with Sam over to Porter Creek restaurant where his parents had reserved a private room for dinner. It was a classy steak house with fine dining. They arrived and were seated at a large long table decorated in fall colors complete with candles and name-place cards. After greeting everyone personally, she and Sam sat down at the center of the table.

Susie walked over with a glass of wine and handed it to Alli. "I was up at the bar, so I got you a glass. Not sure what you're having, Sam, so you're on your own."

"Thanks," Alli said and set the glass down. She knew it was a non-alcoholic wine that Alli had brought her, so she didn't have to explain why she wasn't drinking. This among many other reasons was why Susie was her best friend!

Sam nodded at Susie, then stood up. "I'll be right back," he said and walked over to the bar.

"It's the one you prefer." Susie smiled and took her seat next to Alli.

"You're the best. Thanks for looking out for me."

The appetizers and dinner were superb. The steak she'd ordered was so tender it practically melted in her mouth. In fact, everything was incredible. For dessert, she ordered the Chocolate Molten Lava Cake and it tasted like heaven.

Before she knew it, dinner was over, and everyone was saying their goodbyes. Tomorrow was the big day and she wanted to be well rested. It was only ten but she wanted to get to bed early. She originally intended to go back to her place, but Sam had insisted she spend the night with him.

Later in bed after they'd made love, she lay wrapped up in his arms finally relaxing and her anxiety dissipating. Sam making love to her had been exactly what she'd needed. Within minutes, she was asleep in his arms.

CHAPTER 28

"Sure am glad we opted for a five o'clock wedding." Sam tenderly caressed her cheek with his finger.

"We still have to get up at a decent time," she said as she snuggled closer to him.

"What could you possibly have to do that's more important than lying in bed with me?"

"Do you want a list of what needs to be done this morning?" She rolled over on his chest.

"Not really, but I'm sure you're going to tell me anyway."

"We need to decorate the church, I need to get over to the salon to meet the girls for our hair appointments and our mani-pedis…"

"Okay, I'm getting up. You sent me my list, so I know what I need to do."

"Pick up the rings, help decorate, etc."

"Do you have all the honeymoon reservation confirmations?"

"Yes."

"Do you want to stop for breakfast on the way to the church?"

"Definitely. May be all we get to eat before the reception."

After they'd showered and dressed, they left to have breakfast after a quick stop at Alli's apartment to pick up the decorations and her wedding dress.

At nine-thirty, they met the bridal party and their parents at the church to decorate. With so many people helping, it went quickly and then they all drove over to The Wilds Golf Club to decorate for the reception.

Shortly before noon, all the ladies left for the salon that had been reserved totally for them. Sam's mom was treating everyone to the deluxe pedicure and manicures along with having their hair styled in up-dos. The salon provided mini deli sandwiches and cold salads with a variety of different brownie flavors.

At two o'clock, a limo arrived to take them to the church where the men would be waiting. The women exited the limo and made their way inside to a large room that was used for bridal parties. The dresses were hanging on a coat rack, including the wedding dress.

Alli paused for a moment to take it all in. This was it. This was her wedding day that she'd been waiting for practically her whole life. She was actually getting married and to the love of her life, Sam.

"Alli, you okay?" her mom asked.

"Yes, can't believe I'm actually getting married today."

"Yes, it may seem a little bit surreal right now. Let's get you into that beautiful dress hanging over there," her mom said pointing at the rack.

Alli began undressing, as all the bridesmaids were shedding their clothes, also. Soon, her mom and Susie were holding the dress for her to step into. As it was pulled up and into place, she saw her reflection in the mirror. The dress was striking.

"Oh, Alli, it's so perfect for you." Her mom had tears in her eyes.

"You make such a beautiful bride," Susie said stepping beside Alli to see the reflection in the mirror.

The girl from the salon had met them at the church to help with the veil and to make sure there weren't any hair emergencies. She placed the veil on Alli's head and began pinning it in place with many bobby-pins to make sure it stayed where it was supposed to.

Alli wore a half-carat diamond pendant on a gold chain, her gift from Sam. The one he'd given to her on Christmas a couple of years ago and the one she'd worn almost every day since they'd gotten back together... it was the necklace she'd picked to wear with her wedding dress.

Knocking could be heard from the hallway, so, Sam's mother went to the door to see who was looking for them. It was the photographer ready to take a few pictures.

Alli's phone was on the table beeping that a message had arrived. She picked it up. It was from Sam, 'I love you. See you at 5.' God, she loved him so much.

At four-thirty, the group of ladies headed to the back of the church. Everyone except Alli and her mother. The guests had been already seated.

Fifteen minutes later, her dad knocked on the door. "Alli, are you ready?" he asked after being escorted inside by her mother.

"Yes."

"You look beautiful. I can't believe my baby is getting married." His eyes began to water a little bit.

"Thanks, Dad."

He swiped at his eyes. "Let's do this." He held out his arm for her and the three of them left the room.

Her mom was ushered down the aisle to the front pew, and then the bridesmaids took the arms of the groomsmen as the music changed for the bridal party's entrance which was a queue for them to begin their walk down the aisle to the front of the church.

Alli could now see Sam standing in the front of the church waiting for her. She smiled. Then, the music changed to the wedding march.

She nodded to her dad and they began the long walk to the front of the church where he would give his daughter's care over to Sam. They stopped and Sam put his arm out for Alli to help her up the steps. They turned to face each other in front of the pastor while Susie straightened out the train of her dress.

The pastor began the service, the songs of love were sung by their singer, Angie. Next, they exchanged the vows they'd written and then the rings. Before she knew it, the pastor pronounced them man and wife then Sam kissed her. It had all gone so quickly almost as if it was a blur in her mind.

After Sam and Alli greeted everyone in the line, they and the bridal party went back into the church for photos of them and their parents. When they were done, the limo left to take the bridal party to The Wilds Golf Club for the reception where the guests were already waiting.

As soon as the bridal party arrived, the appetizers were served. The photographer then escorted the bride and groom over to the wedding cake for pictures.

Finally, Alli and Sam were seated at the bridal table and dinner was served. Susie was seated next to Alli, she handed Alli a glass of champagne and nodded. Alli took this to mean Susie had managed to get a glass of non-alcoholic champagne for her. Alli mouthed the words—*Thank you.* She was really glad the not drinking charade would be over soon and she could simply tell Sam the truth in Vegas.

Both Susie and Dustin gave their toasts about the happy couple, bringing up funny stories from the past. Her dad also gave a toast, which prompted Sam's dad to give one, too. Neither her or Sam ate much before the music began playing and it was time to start the first dance for the bride and groom.

They'd both taken ballroom dance classes so the waltz was performed exquisitely and had the crowd clapping.

When it was done, Sam kissed her right smack in the middle of the dance floor. More clapping began. "I love this woman so much!" he exclaimed.

It now became a roar of clapping as the second song began and the bridal party joined them on the dance floor. Soon, their parents were dancing, also. The night progressed as she danced with many of her guests. Later, the music changed to more of the current hits and she danced with her bridesmaids.

The older crowd began leaving as it neared eleven. Their friends who were mostly the younger group stayed to drink and dance. She was extremely glad Susie had kept her glass filled with the non-alcoholic champagne even though she eventually, switched over to simply ice water.

Their parents loaded up the gifts in their SUVs to keep overnight. Finally, pretty much only the bridal party was left, so Sam and Alli left Susie and Dustin to take care of closing everything up at The Wilds Golf Club.

Sam had been drinking the whole night, so Alli didn't want him to drive. "I can drive."

"I can, I'm fine," Sam said.

"No, I switched to water over a couple of hours ago. I will."

"Can you even drive in that dress?" Sam was nuzzling her neck, making it hard for her to even concentrate.

"Of course. I'll just pull it up. It's not like I still have the train attached."

"Okay, Mrs. Cavera." He took her hand and they walked out to his SUV.

She'd forgotten that it would be hard to step up into the SUV though with her dress. Sam finally lifted her into the driver's seat. It was so hilarious that they were both laughing, which led to more kissing. Finally, they put their seat belts on and headed to Sam's place.

Sam insisted on carrying her inside which proved more difficult than he'd thought as he tried to get his arms around all the fabric, but he did it. As soon as they were inside, he kicked the door shut with his foot and took his Tux jacket off. The bow tie and bun were off already, much earlier in the evening.

Alli set her bag down and started taking the bobby pins out of her veil. There were so many of them. Even with Sam helping, it took a bit and his patience was wearing thin. Finally, it fell to the floor. She walked slowly toward the bedroom, Sam following close behind her with a boyish grin on his face. His desire for her was obvious, as she was amazed to see it since this was definitely not their first time.

"You're going to have to help me get out of this dress," she said and turned her back to him.

Shortly, the dress fell to the floor after it was unzipped and unbuttoned. She now stood inside an ivory circle of satin with only her sexy ivory lace bra and thong adorning her spray tanned body.

Swiftly, Sam lifted her up and set her on the bed, then immediately stripped his clothes off to join her. He took his time absolutely adoring every inch of her body with caresses and kisses before bringing her to ecstasy.

Once she was writhing beneath him, he joined her in a paradise they could share. Only the two of them. Forever.

CHAPTER 29

*A*lli woke the next morning to Sam carrying in a tray with breakfast. His fluffy buttermilk pancakes, bacon, eggs and a bowl of fruit. After setting hers down in front of her, he returned with another tray for himself and joined her in bed.

He was being so wonderful to her, she hoped it wouldn't change after she told him about the baby. Oh well, might as well enjoy it while she could.

After breakfast, they showered and dressed for the gift opening hosted by Sam's parents at their house. The bridal party was invited also and it appeared everyone had already arrived when they pulled in the driveway.

It was his parents' house, so they walked in without knocking.

"So, you two made it!" Dustin walked over and gave a half hug to Sam.

"You look radiant," Susie said to Alli walking over.

"Come on in, you two," Sam's dad said. "Have a seat and let's get started. You have quite a lot of gifts to open."

His mom walked over to give Sam and Alli a hug then pointed to a loveseat that had been saved for them. They could hardly get to it with all the gifts stacked in front of it. "We have Mimosa or plain orange juice. Which would you like?"

"I'll take a Mimosa. Thanks Mom," Sam answered.

"Orange juice for me," Alli said.

Susie entered the gift givers names in the cards and also wrote them in the Brides Gift List Book as they opened the gifts.

Dustin boxed everything back up and stacked them up by the wall.

Alli loved their little group. Her girlfriends had been beside her through high school and college. Same with Sam's friends, they'd been college buddies. Sam's parents had been wonderful and treated her like family from the time they'd started dating. She'd been worried that they may have resented her for breaking up with Sam, but they'd welcomed her back with open arms. His mom had been hoping for grandchildren for a while now, so she was going to be happy to hear the news. Her parents had always been there for her and she loved them so much, so it had been hard for her when they'd moved away.

They'd finished up by three o'clock, said their goodbyes and left for the airport to catch their six o'clock flight to Vegas. The gifts would stay at his parent's house until they got back to Minneapolis. Their friends and families had been extremely generous and they'd received so many wonderful gifts.

Shortly after six that evening, their plane took off and they were on their way to Vegas. Alli was feeling extremely agitated at this point. She'd gone over how she would tell Sam in her mind about a million times and she still had no idea how she was going to do it or when. Finally, she fell asleep and so did Sam as he had booked them in First Class and the seats were big and comfortable.

When they arrived in Vegas, it was seven o'clock but it was nine o'clock in Minneapolis. They checked in for their car rental and were on their way to the Bellagio Hotel. Sam had the car valet parked and they walked into the lobby to check in for their room.

"The keys to your suite," the clerk said.

Alli smiled at Sam. "Wow! Didn't know you booked a suite.""

"Compliments of my parents." He took her hand as the bellman followed them to the elevator.

Their room was on the 30th floor and overlooked the strip. Alli was in shock when she walked in. The suite was enormous and had a separate bedroom. It looked as big as her apartment, if not bigger.

The bellman left after setting their bags in the bedroom and receiving a tip from Sam.

She went over to the window to take in the shining lights from the Las Vegas strip. It really did look beautiful. Their room also had a view of the famous Bellagio fountains. Sam walked up behind her and put his arms around her waist. They stood in silence for a few moments.

Alli then turned toward him. "We need to talk." She walked over to the couch and sat down at an angle so she could face him when he joined her.

"You sound serious. What do you want to talk about?"

"Well, I've been thinking about this for a while now. It's probably best to start at the very beginning."

"Is everything okay, Alli?"

"Hopefully, but it depends on you."

"You're being extremely confusing. What do you want to talk about?"

"Do you remember why we broke up?"

"Of course. You wanted a full commitment. Marriage."

"That's part of it."

"Alli, we're married now."

"There was more to the break up than that. Remember the part about children?"

"Yes. Do we have to talk about that now?" He tried to lean over to kiss her.

She held her hands up to stop him. "Yes. But let's go back to getting married first. The last time we were in Vegas, I vaguely remember going to a Wedding Chapel. When you left, you didn't say anything about us getting married, so I didn't think too much about it. Besides, I'd always thought they weren't real or at least they weren't really legal marriages."

"Alli—"

She again held her hand up. "Imagine my surprise when I acciden-tally happened to see a file on your desk labeled Marriage License and when I opened it there was a Las Vegas marriage license with both our signatures. Mind you, I still thought it wasn't real until I looked it up on the internet and found out it definitely was legal and we were already married."

"Alli—" he tried again.

"Even more surprising was that states don't share marriage files, so that's why no one said anything when we filed for the Minnesota marriage license."

"I'm so sorry, Alli. I should've told you, but I wanted to see how things were going to work out first. Then, I didn't want to lose you again, so I didn't say anything because I wanted to be married to you and do it the right way, so you could have your big wedding that you always wanted."

Alli shook her head. "I'm not done yet. I went off the pill when we broke up because I didn't need any type of birth control since I wasn't sleeping with anyone and my doctor thought it would be good to give my body a break."

"But you told me we were safe to have sex without using condoms." Sam now stood up and began pacing the floor.

"At that time it was."

"Alli…"

Alli stood and picked up her jacket off the table. Then she grabbed her purse and placed the strap over her shoulder. She stared at Sam whose face now appeared ashen and confused. "Sam, after I finish telling you what I need you to know, I'm going to go for a walk to think about us and our future. I want you to think about what I say. Take it to heart and decide what you want to do. I don't really want you to say anything now. If you still want to be married to me after what I tell you and you've really thought about it, meet me in front of the fountains at eleven o'clock tonight."

Sam didn't say a word…he simply waited to hear what she had to say.

"First, let me say I've wanted to be married to you ever since the first day we met. When we ran into each other in Vegas, I was leery to say the least. I figured you were looking for some crazy hot sex for old times' sake. For the record, sex with you has always been great. Then you left in the morning and I didn't know what to think. Would you call or wouldn't you call?"

"I said I would call and I did."

"Yes, you did. Then when you actually proposed, I was ecstatic. But that all changed when I realized we already got married in Vegas. So is that why you proposed? Because we were already married?"

"No. I want to be married to you, Alli." Sam moved toward Alli.

She put her hand up for him to stop right where he was standing. "Before that happened, I went to the doctor to get a new prescription for the Pill, but much to my surprise she informed me I was pregnant, so that would be a 'No' for the Pill."

Sam stared at her as a look of momentary horror crossed his face.

"I didn't tell you because I didn't want you to call off the wedding. I wanted my baby to have a father and mother who were married. I know that may sound old-fashioned, but that's the way I think. So then when I found out we were already married, I figured it didn't matter one way or the other. Why call off the wedding at that point, right?"

He didn't answer.

"So we are double married, I'm pregnant and divorces are basically as easy in Vegas as the weddings are, or so I've heard."

"You got pregnant that night in Vegas?"

"Yes, it appears so." She went over to the door and opened it. "Sam, I love you, but you need to love me and the baby or I will make a go of it on my own." She walked out the door and it closed behind her.

Alli took the elevator to the lobby area and spotted a bench outside a garden area where she sat down and let the tears she'd been holding back for too long flow freely down her cheeks.

CHAPTER 30

Sam sat down at the dining table and slammed his fist down hard on it. "What the hell just happened?"

All he could think of was that she was pregnant with his child. It was never that he didn't want children, it just totally scared the hell out of him to be a father. He had no doubt that Alli would be a great mother. She'd always loved children.

Did she really think he'd want a divorce because she was pregnant? Well, he could kind of understand she might think that, considering the break up and all. He ran his fingers through his hair. He'd really messed things up! He knew he should've told her about the Vegas wedding right away, but no, he'd wanted to play it safe in case they didn't work everything out and get back together.

She definitely had every right to not tell him about the baby. How could he even be mad at her? It wasn't her fault he'd gotten her pregnant. If it was anyone's fault, it was definitely his fault. He should've used a condom. She'd been on the pill forever though, so he hadn't even given it a second thought. Plus, he'd had way too much to drink that night. But not too much that he didn't know what he was doing.

He looked at his phone to check the time, it was only a little after nine o'clock. What was he supposed to do for two hours? Now that he was going to be a dad, it actually felt like a huge load had been lifted off his shoulders. He didn't have to make the decision, it had already been made for him. He would be having a family with Alli and he actually smiled.

With his nervous energy, he unpacked their suitcases, took a shower. He dressed in some fresh clothes, then left the room. Once the elevator reached the lobby, he looked for a flower shop where he purchased a bouquet of a dozen white roses. Then he went into a gift shop that sold baby and children's items. He looked around until he found a plush ivory baby blanket that would be perfect for Alli. Well, not for Alli but for the baby. On the wall, he saw a T-shirt hanging that said Father-to-be and a matching Mother-to-be. He bought all three items and had them wrapped and put in a large baby bag which could also hold the roses.

It was now ten-thirty, so he decided he would just be early and walked out to the fountains. She hadn't specified where though and it was a large area, so he picked a spot in the middle. Hopefully, she would see him there. He watched the couples passing by and the families with children even out at this late hour. Out of habit, he took out his phone and was so tempted to call her, but he knew he needed to wait.

Out of the corner of his eye, he saw Alli seated on a bench back on the grassy area. She looked like she was crying. He hated it when she cried. And he knew he was the cause of those tears. *To hell with waiting!* He walked toward her.

She had her head bent down, so she didn't see him approach.

Sam stopped in front of her holding the baby bag in front of him. "Alli."

She looked up with her tear stained face that showed signs of a smile beginning to form as she focused on the baby bag he was holding.

He handed it to her. She took it from him as he sat down next to her. "Alli, I'm so sorry." He put his arm around her and she laid her head on his shoulder. "I love you and I will love our baby, too."

Alli leaned up to kiss him. "Sam, I was so worried you wouldn't want me or the baby."

"I'm not going to deny that being a dad scares the hell out of me. But because I know you will be a great mother, I know that you will help me to be the best father I can possibly be. And as for you, I'm never letting you go again. I love you and can't imagine spending my life without you."

"I love you, Sam."

"Open the bag."

Alli opened it and started crying again, when she saw the T-shirts, blanket and roses. Only this time they were tears of joy. "How about we go back to the room?" she asked.

As they began walking back, the hotel's water fountains, along with music, began performing their spectacular show, so they stopped to watch the display.

When it finished, they returned to the room where a luxurious king size bed awaited them.

EPILOGUE

On a snowy day at the end of March, Alli laid in bed contemplating getting up to make her way to the bathroom again. She'd only managed a few hours of sleep during the night since there basically wasn't a position that felt comfortable with a stomach as large as hers. Sam had been so wonderful taking care of her this last week. He'd taken time off work to be with her since the due date was now past and the baby could come at any time.

Sam was still asleep, so she awkwardly managed to get up out of the bed to a standing position and walk to the bathroom. Almost immediately after turning on the light, she felt a rush of water running down her legs, making a huge puddle on the floor.

She had promised herself that she wouldn't panic, but she did. "Sam! Wake up!"

Sam instantly sat up in bed, then stood and rushed toward her. "Are you okay?"

"Yes. My water broke and we need to go to the hospital now!"

Sam frantically searched for his pants and shirt. He then paused and glanced her way.

Alli could see he was in panic mode. "Start the car, then help me get dressed."

Once they were in the car and on their way, Alli called her mom who would meet them at the hospital with her dad and she also promised to call Sam's parents.

"Alli, are you okay?" he asked.

"Yes. Just keep driving."

At the hospital, Sam stayed with her the whole twelve hours of labor, comforting her and talking her through the breathing exercises they had practiced in the birthing classes.

Sam finally was holding his newborn daughter and his love for this tiny little baby was obvious. He laid the baby down beside Alli. "So Addison it is." He smiled.

"But we'll call her Addi," Alli commented. "How are you doing, Sam?"

"Me, I'm fine. I didn't just deliver a baby."

"I love you, Sam." Alli reached out to hold his hand.

"I love you so much and I was terrified that I could lose you and the baby if something went wrong."

"But we're both doing great. I just need you to relax, at least a little bit." She now understood where his fear of having children stemmed from.

The nurse walked into the room and asked, "Both of your parents are waiting to come in. Should I let them in?"

"Of course," Alli said.

"Both your grandmothers are very excited to see you, Addi," Sam said to the baby.

The four parents entered the room with smiles beaming. The two grandmothers, especially, had been waiting a long time for this moment.

Alli had, too. The day had finally arrived and she couldn't be happier, especially to see Sam's instant love for their daughter.

They were now a family—Sam, Alli and Addi.

RECIPE

CHOCOLATE ALMOND CAKE

Ingredients

Cake

- 3/4 cup butter, softened
- 1-2/3 cups sugar
- 2 large eggs
- 3/4 cup sour cream
- 1 teaspoon vanilla extract
- 1 teaspoon almond extract
- 2 cups all-purpose flour
- 2/3 cup baking cocoa
- 2 teaspoons baking soda
- 1/2 teaspoon salt
- 1 cup buttermilk

Frosting

- 5 tablespoons butter, softened
- 2-1/2 cups confectioners' sugar

- 1 teaspoon vanilla extract
- 1/2 teaspoon almond extract
- 3 to 4 tablespoons whole milk
- Sliced almonds, toasted

Directions

1. In a large bowl, cream butter and sugar. Add eggs, beat well. Add sour cream and extracts; mix well. Combine flour, cocoa, baking soda and salt; add to the creamed mixture alternately with buttermilk, beating well after each addition.

2. Pour into a greased 10-in. fluted tube pan. Bake at 350° until a toothpick inserted in the center comes out clean, 50-55 minutes. Cool for 10 minutes before removing from pan to a wire rack to cool completely.

3. For frosting, cream butter, sugar and extracts in a small bowl until smooth. Add milk until frosting reaches desired spreading consistency. Spread over cake. Decorate with almonds.

ABOUT THE AUTHOR

Rose Marie Meuwissen, a first-generation Norwegian American born and raised in Minnesota, always tries to incorporate her Norwegian heritage into her writing. After receiving a BA in Marketing from Concordia University, a Masters in Creative Writing from Hamline University soon followed. Minnesota is still where she calls home.

She has traveled around the world, including Scandinavia, but still has many places to see, enjoys attending Scandinavian events, writing conferences and is usually busy writing Minnesota Lakes Contemporary Romances, Viking Time Travel Romances or Norwegian Traditions Children's Books.

Visit her at www.rosemariemeuwissen.com or www.realnorwegianseatlutefisk.com.

NOVELS:

- *Taking Chances*—a contemporary romance novel set in Minnesota and Arizona.
- *Married by Saturday*—a contemporary romance novel set in Minnesota and Montana.
- *Accidental Vegas Bride*—a contemporary romance novel set in Minnesota and Nevada.
- *Looking for Mr. Right*—a contemporary internet dating romance novel set on Prior Lake in Minnesota—*Coming soon!*

NOVELLAS:

- *Annika—A Christmas Romance*—a contemporary romance set in Minnesota with a Nordic theme during the Christmas Holidays.
- *Skol! Viking Blonde Ale*—a contemporary romance set in Minnesota at an Autumn festival complete with a fortune teller, ale and Vikings!
- *Choosing to Live*—a Norwegian woman's journey during WWII to survive the Nazi Occupation of Norway—*Coming soon!*

MINNESOTA LAKES ROMANCE NOVELETTES:

- *A Kiss Under the Northern Lights*—a Summer romance set in Ely, Minnesota on Big Lake.
- *Dancing in the Moonlight*—a Summer romance set in Malmo, Minnesota on Mille Lacs Lake.
- *Hot Summer Nights*—a Summer romance set in Prior Lake, Minnesota on Prior Lake.
- *Railroad Ties*—an Autumn romance set in Two Harbors, Minnesota on Lake Superior.
- *Blizzard of Love*—a Winter romance set in Lutsen, Minnesota on Lake Superior.
- *A Norwegian Gift of Love*—a Spring romance set in Minneapolis, Minnesota on Lake Harriet.
- *Old Yule Log Fires*—a Christmas romance set in Excelsior, Minnesota on Lake Minnetonka.
- *A Date for Valentine's Day*—a Valentine romance set in Minnetonka Beach, Minnesota at the Lafayette Country Club on Lake Minnetonka.
- *Dance of Love*—a Fall Festival romance set at the Renaissance Fair in Shakopee, Minnesota.

CHILDREN'S BOOKS—REAL NORWEGIAN'S SERIES:

- *Real Norwegians Eat Lutefisk*—a Children's book about the tradition of Lutefisk presented in both English and Norwegian.
- *Real Norwegians Eat Rømmegrøt*—the second Children's book in the series about the tradition of Rømmegrøt presented in both English and Norwegian.
- *Real Norwegians Eat Lefse*—the third Children's book in the series about the tradition of Lefse presented in both English and Norwegian.
- *Real Norwegians Eat Krumkake*—the fourth Children's book in the series about the tradition of Krumkake presented in both English and Norwegian—*Coming next!*

MICRO-MINI NOVELETTE—COMING SOON!

- *Christmas Notes*—a collection of Christmas prose poems to warm the heart during the Christmas season.

CONTINUE READING FOR A PREVIEW OF:

SKOL! VIKING BLONDE ALE

Fortunes, Love & Fate Series

CONTINUE READING FOR A PREVIEW OF:

Rose Marie Meuwissen

SKOL! VIKING BLONDE ALE

COPYRIGHT

Skol! Viking Blonde Ale

Fortunes, Love & Fate Series
Print Edition
Copyright 2020 by Rose Marie Meuwissen

SKOL! VIKING BLONDE ALE

ISBN 978-0-9903788-3-9
Published in the United States of America
Nordic Publishing LLC
Cover Design by Raine English

SKOL! VIKING BLONDE ALE

FORTUNES, LOVE & FATE SERIES

Inga was living the dream, planning events for her own company, Unique Events, but she still hadn't found a guy who could be 'The One' for her. She never would've believed a fortune from a gypsy fortune teller promising her a 'love that surpasses time' could come true.

Erik moved from Norway to Minnesota to expand his Nordic Brewing company in the U. S. He'd promised himself to devote all his time to the business, but how was he to know that an unknown force of fate would introduce him to a woman he couldn't walk away from?

Their attraction could not be denied because ultimately, they were destined to be together. But could the Atlantic Ocean keep them apart? Would that even be possible if they were truly soul mates?

INGA'S FORTUNE:

Someone from your past will reappear in your life.
Your true soul mate.
With him, you will experience a love that surpasses time.

PROLOGUE

James J. Hill Days in Wayzata
Lake Minnetonka
September

Inga pulled into the back-parking lot of Main Street Books at six. She couldn't believe it wasn't later. Friday night rush hour traffic on the 494 Freeway was bumper to bumper all the way from Eden Prairie to Wayzata. The weather was still holding its summer like temps and true Minnesotans would never pass up a beautiful autumn weekend to go up North to their cabins one last time before winter arrived. Today was the James J. Hill Days celebration in Wayzata and the main street was packed with people as she made her way into the book store to find her *Romancing the Lakes of Minnesota* book club. This month instead of their regular meeting, they planned to enjoy walking around and checking out the celebration. Probably was a good call, she thought, since it would've been difficult to hold their meeting in the crowded book store and the activity outside would've been immensely distracting.

"Am I the last one to arrive?" Inga asked as she approached the book club group standing in front of the latest arrival shelf where the romance section was located.

"Bet the traffic was awful," Nora stated.

"Ready, to brave the crowds?" Katie asked.

"I'm hungry and thirsty, let's go!" Violet said.

Inga nodded in agreement and followed the group out the door to Main Street. They made their way down the street stopping at booths to look at the novelties for sale until finally, they stopped at the end of the street where the most unusual trailer was parked. The sign above the open door read, 'Fortune Teller'. It appeared to be Vintage, but these days they could make anything look old, even if it was new. Although, she had to admit, she'd never seen anything like it before, even though she'd been to many events. After all, she was an event planner. Intrigued was putting it mildly. Unfortunately, there was no stopping her curiosity. So, she entered the trailer.

"Come in, please," a very thickly accented voice beckoned from inside the trailer.

"Hello." Inga ducked and stepped into the trailer, taking in all the antiques and draped surroundings.

"Take a seat," the lady in gypsy like garb directed. "Let me see what your life has in store for you."

Inga didn't believe in fortune telling, at least she didn't think she did, but what could it possibly hurt to oblige the lady. It might be worth a laugh later, so she sat down on the partially pulled out chair at the table.

The fortune teller took the seat across from Inga and reached for her hand.

Slowly, Inga extended her hand. When their hands touched, Inga felt a strange sensation flow through her entire body, almost like a spark of electricity. It only lasted a few seconds and then was gone. She had no idea what it was or what caused it, but she finally relaxed.

The woman's face seemed deep in thought and completely fixated on her hand. "You are a very special lady. Very strong and independent. I see happiness in your future."

"Do you see a man?" Inga wasn't sure why'd she'd asked that particular question.

"Yes." The woman continued staring at her hand. "A very handsome man."

"Well, there certainly are enough good-looking men around. What I need is one that is interested in me long enough to stick around for a while."

"You have not met '*The One*' yet."

"When? When will it happen? I'm getting really tired of waiting around for him."

"Soon."

"So, is that my fortune?"

"No." The woman hesitated, then picked up a piece of paper and wrote a few lines down on it. She handed it to Inga. "This is your fortune: *Someone from your past will reappear in your life. Your true soul mate. With him, you will experience a love that surpasses time.*"

"Great. But I'm sorry, I don't believe in magic."

"That's okay you don't have to believe. It will happen anyway."

Their eyes locked for a moment.

Inga got up to leave. "How much do I owe you?" Inga asked.

"For you, no charge. I've been waiting for you."

"I don't understand."

The fortune teller waived her hand in a shooing motion, indicating Inga was done and should leave.

As Inga stepped out of the trailer, Katie rushed up the steps. "My turn."

"So, what do you think? Is the Fortune Teller legit?" Violet asked.

"What kind of a question is that? Of course, it's not real. No one can tell another person what will happen in their future," Stephanie said.

"Care to share?" Nora asked.

Inga handed the piece of paper to Violet, who in turn handed it to Stephanie, who in turn handed it to Gwen and lastly to Nora.

"At least it's a good fortune. Let's hope it comes true," Stephanie said.

"Come on, you're not buying into this stuff, are you?" Inga shook her head.

Minutes later, Katie came down the trailer's steps, paper in hand grinning from ear to ear.

Violet practically ran to the steps to be next.

Each romance book club member shared their fortune while the next one took their turn. Being romantics at heart, they were all thrilled to find romance in their fortunes.

They continued strolling leisurely down the other side of the street where the craft brewery tents were located.

Inga spotted a tent with *Nordic Brewing* as the name. She selected it out of the five tents because of her love for all things Nordic and Viking. In fact, the Viking Ship logo caught her eye first. She walked up to the counter to see the menu more closely.

"What can I get you?"

Inga looked up quickly when she heard the strong Norwegian accented English and to her surprise saw almost a *'Thor'* look alike, only his blonde hair was shorter. He could very well be from Viking blood, she thought. *Tall, muscular, with a chiseled face. Have I just died and gone to Valhalla?*

"What can I get you?" he repeated smiling broadly at her.

"What would you suggest?" she managed to get out. "I've never tried your brand before."

"For you lovely lady, I'd suggest the Viking Blonde Ale."

"Sounds absolutely perfect."

He turned his broad toned back toward her stretching the black T-shirt taut against his muscles and filled a plastic souvenir cup with Valhalla printed on one side and a picture of a Viking on the other side.

Inga pulled a five-dollar bill from her purse and set it on the counter. He handed her the cup instead of setting it down and her fingers lightly brushed his in the process. *There it was again.* A shiver of sorts shimmied its way through her body.

"Thank you, hope you enjoy it," he said as he picked up the money to put in the cash register.

"Thanks, I'm sure I will," Inga said while her eyes lingered on this modern-day Viking man. She felt sad that she would most likely not ever see him again. *Oh well, one can only wish.* She turned and walked away spotting her friends up ahead at a different craft brewery tent.

www.ingramcontent.com/pod-product-compliance
Lightning Source LLC
Chambersburg PA
CBHW032013240626
47153CB00003B/1240